ARCANE AGE™

How the Mighty are Fallen

by slade

Author: slade
Editor: Jim Butler
Project Coordinator: Thomas M. Reid
Concept: Mark Anthony, Jim Butler, Julia Martin, Steven Schend, and Jim Ward
Cover Illustrator: Nick Jainschigg
Interior Illustrator: Ned Dameron
Graphic Designer: Dee Barnett
Art Coordinator: Bob Galica
Typesetting: Tracey L. Isler
Prepress Coordinator: Dave Conant
Playtesters: Deneen Olsen (DM); John Creech, Robby Duncan, Eran Edwards, Rich Jenkins, Dave Kelsay, Leonard McGillis, Jeff Pashke, Marty Ruger, Ethan Schazenbach, and Victor Semlek

TSR, Inc.
201 Sheridan Springs Rd
Lake Geneva,
WI 53147
U. S. A.

TSR Ltd.
120 Church End
Cherry Hinton
Cambridge, CB1 3LB
United Kingdom

ADVANCED DUNGEONS & DRAGONS, AD&D, DUNGEON MASTER, FORGOTTEN REALMS, SPELLJAMMER, and the TSR logo are registered trademarks owned by TSR, Inc. ARCANE AGE, and ENCYCLOPEDIA MAGICA are trademarks owned by TSR, Inc. All TSR characters, character names and the distinctive likenesses thereof are trademarks owned by TSR, Inc. Distributed to the book trade in the United States by Random House, Inc. and in Canada by Random House of Canada Ltd. Distributed to the toy and hobby trade by regional distributors. Distributed in the United Kingdom by TSR Ltd. This FORGOTTEN REALMS game accessory is protected under the copyright laws of the United States of America and other countries. Any reproduction or unauthorized use of the material or artwork printed herein is prohibited without the express written permission of TSR, Inc. Copyright ©1996 TSR, Inc. All rights reserved. Made in the U.S.A.

TABLE OF CONTENTS

THE TIME HAS COME

now ye the events before they shall come to pass. Let them lend thy heart to gladness and ease for in them ye shall know the future and nigh thine heart to concern.

This Adventure

How the Mighty are Fallen allows player-characters the opportunity to participate in the final days of Netheril. Characters are given the opportunity to aid in the empire's destruction or seek to prevent what must come to pass. The *Netheril: Empire of Magic* boxed set is required to fully utilize the adventures within these pages.

Abbreviations

Some of the abbreviations used within this product might confuse novice DMs during the course of play. These include:

NPC short-form descriptions, such as Karsus (CN hm A41): The first two letters in parentheses refer to alignment (chaotic neutral), the middle two refer to race and sex (human male), and the final letter and number refer to class and level (41st-level arcanist). An extensive list of these are included in the FORGOTTEN REALMS® *Campaign Setting*.

A#: Arcanists are the wizards of Netheril. Complete information on them can be found in the *Netheril: Empire of Magic* boxed set.

P#: Priests are likewise detailed in the boxed set. Clerics do not exist in Netheril except as specialty priests.

Notes to the DM

This adventure is not extraordinarily linear in nature; players can choose to follow a variety of paths that lead to the Fall of Netheril. As such, the DM should read the entire adventure and understand the directions that the heroes can take before game play begins.

Additional magical items and spells are included at the end of the adventure. The DM is encouraged to add additional elements from the *Empire of Magic* boxed set to alter the adventure to fit into his own campaign. Encounters with tomb tappers and the sharn are obvious elements that should be considered for inclusion into this adventure.

The DM should be generous with common information if players are running characters who are native to Netheril. Time-traveling characters who jump into Netheril at its Fall should be at a disadvantage in terms of common knowledge, available contacts, and reputation.

Spelljamming is mentioned at several points in this adventure (as well as in the *Empire of Magic* boxed set). Knowledge of the spelljamming vessels, rules, and equipment isn't necessary to run the adventure; it's provided strictly as background for those Dungeon Masters who are currently using the SPELLJAMMER® *Campaign Setting* (#1049) and *Realmspace* (#9312) supplements.

Synopsis

The adventure begins as characters enter the spelljamming city of Yeoman's Loft, the heart of Netheril's Realmspace activities. Here they meet Nopheus, a jeweler who's looking for some adventurers to retrieve the body of his wife from her resting place in the Gods' Legion Mountains. Characters can choose to explore the city, get involved in the thieves' guild, or simply investigating the bargains to be found in the city's many shops.

The heroes can also take a trip to the floating city of Karsus for an opportunity to do some Neth-style shopping in the side trek *Karsus Marketplace*. They can choose to join the constabulary in *Quelling the Serfs* as they attempt to rid the city of rebellious people.

Once all of the enclave business has been taken care of, the party most likely sets out to locate the body of Nopheus's wife, Amanda. Again, though, forces conspire to deter them, this time in the form of a summons by the great Archwizard himself—Karsus. It seems he needs a few spell components, and he thinks that the heroes are just the ones who should undertake **The Search**.

Of course, talking a gold dragon out of its gizzard and asking the Tarrasque for its pituitary gland are not easy tasks. It'll take more than a strong sword arm before the characters can get back on task to locate Amanda.

When the characters enter **The Graveyard** they encounter some elves who're disturbed by the complete loss of dead bodies—they've all been dug up and carried off. According to the map that Nopheus gave them, Amanda's grave was here somewhere. Hopefully, with little prompting from the elves and the DM, the characters are soon **On the Trail of the Dead**, the real meat of the adventure.

They encounter their first undead in Faerûn's past and are probably be surprised to find that the zombie is intelligent and can carry on a conversation—and probably a tune if asked. If they assist the zombie and help mend his fractured leg, they make themselves an ally that might just save their life later on in the adventure.

While following the trail of the undead, the heroes run into a berserk ranger who's grieving over the loss of his family and friends. If the characters resist the urge to swing their swords, they make another friend. As their friend departs on a mission of his own, the sounds of **The Orc Retreat** greet their ears. The furor is just an army of orcs running from something terrifying. A captured orc gives the characters their first report of an opponent known as the Lichlord.

If the characters are carrying any magical items, they attract the attention of the phaerimm, who have extreme prejudice against humans (especially Netherese) and their gluttonous use of magic. The phaerimm gate into the scene to attack the owners, hoping to steal the magic as well as a few of the humans carrying them. If they manage to capture one or more of the characters, the phaerimm carry them down into the Underdark to their mind flayer comrades. There, **The Elusive Illithid** delves into their minds to excavate any information. Escape is not impossible— though fate may prove kinder to them should they stay. The **Dead's Denizens**, in the form of three evil and cruel arcanists sent by the Lichlord himself ambush the characters. This can be used as a major clue that the characters are getting too close in the eyes of the Lichlord.

As they near the end of the adventure, they come across an eerie castle—one constructed of the bodies of skeletons and zombies. This is the home of **The Lichlord** himself. Thousands of corpses form the walls, floor, and roof, and hundreds more participate every hour as undead flock to the area. The characters, however, are not alone in this adventure. Karsus himself has been preparing for this ever since he first heard of the Lichlord and speculated on his actions. What better but to have the Archwizard himself as your personal ally (even if he is hundreds of miles away) preparing the greatest magical concoction in human history!

The **Epilogue** tells the happenings immediately after the Fall of Netheril.

THE GRAND WELCOME

I n every dawn, the sun welcomes the kind soul to the new day, and in every dusk, the iniquitous souls — unwelcome in the light — dig their way to the surface.

Yeoman's Loft

Lured by reports of great wealth and prosperity, the adventures have just arrived at the city of Yeoman's Loft, the heart of Netheril's spelljamming activities. From here, merchants distribute rare fabrics, ores, and other Realmspace treasures throughout Netheril.

But the people are disgruntled, the result of a lack of food and the continued decadence of the archwizards. Riots, once unheard of in Netheril, are now a regular occurrence. Murder, a sin once viewed as a temporary inconvenience, is now a serious, nightly dilemma that cannot be cured—thanks to the insipid phaerimm and their magic that's laying waste to the fields and streams throughout Netheril.

At the city's main gate, a large wooden sign with a red arrow can't help but attract attention to itself. If the characters inspect the sign, they notice a small wooden box attached to the post which reads "Touch ye here and receive a gazetteer of Yeoman's Loft." If they do so, they receive a small piece of parchment with streets labeled and a few important buildings noted in sepia-toned ink. (See the map on page 7 for a detail of Yeoman's Loft.)

As the players travel through the city, refer to the Yeoman's Loft map. When they approach the corner of Oak and Pleasance, read the following:

The fierce high-noon sun beats down upon the streets and buildings of Yeoman's Loft. To the southwest, huge ships hover in the air as workmen carry goods to and from their holds. Some of the ships look like those you've seen in the Narrow Sea, while others appear almost insect-like in their construction.

Hundreds of people rush about as well. A few have stopped to chat at a nearby street corner while the remainder carry messages, lead heavily laden horses, or just casually stroll along the street. Everywhere, however, can be seen the local militia as they stand guard and scour newcomers to their city. About a dozen guards are throwing your group suspicious stares.

From a shadowed alley stumbles a man dressed in tattered green robes with dirty golden trim. His hair is disheveled and his face shows a few weeks worth of ragged growth. Dark circles highlight his eyes, but he appears to have not so long ago been part of the wealthy.

"Alas," he cries, agonizing tears staining his face. Gazing into the sky, he raises his hands—one of which is clutching a wine bottle—and cries out. "Amaunator, my lord, what did I do to deserve such misfortune? Tyche, have you abandoned me? How is my beloved to come to me now?"

If characters approach the man, the first thing they realize is that he's been drinking for quite a while; the bottle of wine he holds is nearly empty. If they're kind and not threatening, the man explains to them the reasons behind his sorrow.

He introduces himself as Nopheus (NG hm F8), a jeweler by trade. A few months ago, a quasimagical item was implanted in a popular tavern that imitated the effects of a *Noanar's delayed fireball*. Nearly a hundred people were killed in the resulting inferno, including his beloved wife.

Nopheus claims that he spent thousands of gold performing the death rituals and preserving her body for the possibility of a *resurrection*. He saved every coin he could, sold his business and chateau, and released all his servants. After selling the rest of his belongings, he finally had enough to have his wife brought back from the dead, but no one will now help

Adventure Flow

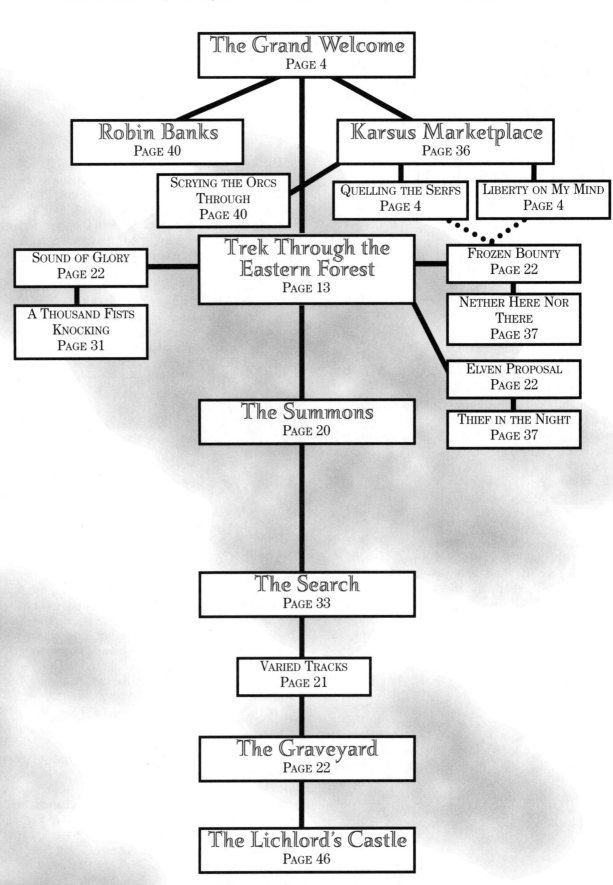

The Grand Welcome
PAGE 4

Robin Banks
PAGE 40

Karsus Marketplace
PAGE 36

Scrying the Orcs
Through
PAGE 40

Quelling the Serfs
PAGE 4

Liberty on My Mind
PAGE 4

Sound of Glory
PAGE 22

Trek Through the
Eastern Forest
PAGE 13

Frozen Bounty
PAGE 22

A Thousand Fists
Knocking
PAGE 31

Nether Here Nor
There
PAGE 37

Elven Proposal
PAGE 22

The Summons
PAGE 20

Thief in the Night
PAGE 37

The Search
PAGE 33

Varied Tracks
PAGE 21

The Graveyard
PAGE 22

The Lichlord's Castle
PAGE 46

Adventure Flow Chart

Gazetteer of Yeoman's Loft

Last Home to Netheril's Thriving Aerocosmologic Community

A. Neth Gatehouse

B. Constable Station

C. Dock Hands' Guildhouse

D. Tavern or Alehouse

E. Hostel or Inn

F. Grocer Cartel

G. General Supply Vendor

H. Bathhouse or Masseuse

I. Courthouse and Jail House

J. Temple of Amaunator

K. Temple of Mystryl

L. Temple of Tyche

M. Shipwright Business

N. Historical Site: Oberon's Laboratory.

O. Spacefarers' Guild

P. Warehouse.

him exhume her body, for they're all too consumed with their own problems.

If the heroes seem interested, Nopheus invites them all back to his house, explaining that he can go into more detail there. Nopheus's house (on the north corner of the intersection) looks run-down. Made of stonework and moldering wood, the window coverings are rotting, hanging by a single hinge, and waving in the slight wind.

Nopheus leads the party into his home and silently closes the door behind him. The furnishings within are very nice but show great wear. All the furniture has small tags with prices attached with straight pins or stuffed into a tight corner to assure they are visible. He offers them a seat before the fireplace in his den.

"My wife, Amanda, was the only possession I cared about. Yes, I had everything a man would want or even care to have, but without her by my side to enjoy it with me, it was all worthless and trite. When she died, I had most of my money tied up in investments. I barely had enough required to have her body preserved and buried. In the intervening months, I've sold my business and valued possessions, liquidated my investments, and rented this shack because it was the cheapest thing I could find. I now have the funds necessary to bring her back to life and to pay those who would help me.

"Everyone seems to be tied up in their own troubles," says Nopheus. "Few are willing to brave the wilds for someone they don't know. I've thought of going out to her gravesite and exhuming her myself, but I'm a jeweler, not an adventurer, so I'm not well-equipped to do battle with orc raiding parties and other ground-dwelling predators.

"I've managed to collect 2,000 gold pieces and have held on to a few magical items that I've collected over the years. Are you interested in doing such a task for me?"

• If the characters demand 2,000 gold per person, he tries to negotiate with 1,000 gold per person plus any furniture or other furnishings still in the house. If they're nonnegotiable, he agrees up to and including 12,000 in gold (and any home furnishings the PCs desire), for that's all he has to spare. Throughout the negotiation process, Nopheus's sword, *Twinrazor*, remains hidden and magically protected from detection under the couch he sits upon. The blade never comes into the equation, and the character cannot detect the blade's presence in any way. See the **Spells & Magic** chapter for information on *Twinrazor*.

• If asked, the money set aside for his wife's resurrection is not in his house, but in a bank here in Yeoman's Loft.

- If the characters look at the map and do not see any banks, he says the banks aren't listed on the tourist maps for security reasons.

- If the party wants to make sure he has the money, the bank Nopheus uses is located on the corner of Shadowtop and Aeroroad.

☞ If the characters decide to rob the bank, refer to **Robin Banks** on page 40.

If they refuse to help him, or it's obvious that he can't work out a deal with them, Nopheus cries out to the gods once again in anguish, cursing Tyche at his poor fortune. The player characters can then continue their exploration of the city; adventure can present itself in many ways. If the characters agree to find his wife, read the following:

"Amanda was buried in the Gods' Legion mountain range several miles to the southeast. I was given permission to bury her in the Shadowtop Clan's holy burial grounds located in the Eastern Forest.

"Here's a map of the general area. Her headstone is a heavy stone tablet with the words, 'Amanda, beloved wife and mother, 3482-3519' etched upon its surface. Inside, you'll see a beautiful woman of 36 years. She has long brunette hair and was buried in a white death gown and wore a necklace with a large blood red ruby surrounded by the silvery web of a black widow. The necklace is unmistakable because it's one of a kind."

The map Nopheus refers to is supplied on page 14 of the adventure. Unfortunately, the characters have to sneak into the funeral grounds in order to exhume the body, but Nopheus "forgets" to tell that to the characters; and the ground is neither consecrated *nor* holy, as discovered later in the adventure.

With that, he bids the characters a fond "fare well and good luck." Proceed to the next chapter, **Trek Through the Eastern Forest**

A. Neth Gatehouse

Netherese gatehouses serve as a port of call for those who seek magical transport to other Netherese cities. Since they're used to seeing a large number of visitors, street merchants and guards make themselves noticeable to passersby.

The courtyard is crammed with small cart vendors selling spell components, altered magical items, and preserved meats. The people here are clothed in the finest clothing you've ever seen. Some people wear robes and cloaks that seem to shimmer with a power of their own, producing prismatic effects across their surfaces. Their hair, perfect in every detail, is neatly combed; the skin is perfectly toned and free of blemishes.

Characters are free to purchase common food, silver pins, and other memorabilia from the city of Yeoman's Loft here. As they wander around the gatehouse area, they notice a series of columns that seem to hold the interest of well-armed individuals.

Carbury's mouth spells etch their way along the surface of a circular row of columns. As the mouths speak their messages, groups of people move from one to the other, listening and taking notes on parchment. Some speak tales of bravery from annals of histories unknown to you, while others spout legal nonsense about the laws of Yeoman's Loft. One set of pale gray lips speaks this message:

"My name is Nopheus. Please help me. My wife was murdered in a vicious attack and I finally have the funds necessary to *resurrect* her.

"I can pay 2,000 pieces of gold, five items of magic, and one *Book of Mythal* to those who would bring her body to me. Please contact me at Yeoman's Loft, on the northern corner of Oak and Pleasance Streets."

If characters proceed to the specified location, refer to the start of this chapter for their encounter with Nopheus.

Another constantly repeating *Carbury's mouth*, also close by, calls out to all in hearing range.

"A call to arms, my friend. We're in dire need! The groundlings are incessantly procuring arms to wield against the archwizards! The magical nature of Netheril requires the constant vigilance of the archwizards to assure everything stays intact. Without their care, Netheril shall come crashing down upon our heads, leaving us open to attack from our ancestral enemies: the orcs and their lackeys.

"For those who wield magic or steel, please register thyself with the Karsus Enclave constabulary to fight in the war against subversion."

If the characters begin searching for a means of travel to the Karsus Enclave, they don't have far to look. A long line of people has formed outside a small wooden building nearby. Guards stand all around this structure, and more guards stand next to an iron strongbox that is being filled with gold one customer at a time.

The guards explain to the patrons that travel to the Karsus Enclave (or any other floating city) costs 50 gold pieces per person. It's roughly a one-hour waiting time for each departure, since they don't want their patrons teleporting onto some cargo (each city follows a specific schedule).

If the characters enter the shack and pay their fee, they arrive in Karsus, slightly disoriented from the journey.

A beautiful landscape stretches out as far as the eye can see. Picturesque, it almost seems that the colors have been modified and intensified. A certain electricity fills the air, causing an immediate sense of activity, excitement, and lucidity in your body.

An island of land hangs in the sky like a minaret with ivy, roots, and waterfalls flowing off its undersides. Buildings of all shapes and sizes reside on the topside of this floating island, but one thing stands clear: The buildings are well cared.

The other travelers that entered the gatehouse with the heroes immediately begin walking toward a small building a few hundred feet away. If the PCs ask, one of the other travelers mutters something about "Scryers making sure we're not an invasion force" and angrily waves his hands into the air.

If the characters approach the building, the door opens and a disembodied voice springs out of nothingness and enters their head.

> "Welcome! Pleasant travels and journeys, friend. Knowledge of the Great Planar Archwizards to ye all."

One thing non-native characters notice immediately is the language difference, a noticeable change in dialect and accent. The accentuation can be picked up and mimicked in 20 weeks (subtract from this time one week per point of Intelligence, eventually giving the character a chance to appear and sound like natives of Netheril).

If the characters enter the building, they reappear in the midst of a busy courtyard. A few people notice their appearance, but think nothing of it, walking past them, their minds focused on their own course. Much like the gatehouse in Yeoman's Loft, numerous peddlers and guards roam the streets here, looking for profits or trouble. Different buildings here promise instantaneous transport to the other enclaves; all for a 50-gp fee, of course.

☞ If the characters enter the marketplace to purchase things, refer to **Karsus Marketplace** on page 36.

☞ If the characters decide to join the constabulary in the fight against the subversive groundlings as told by the second *Carbury's mouth* in Yeoman's Loft, refer to **Quelling the Serfs** side trek on page 37.

B. Constable

The Constable's office serves as the headquarters for law enforcement for the city of Yeoman's Loft. It's a hectic place filled with people with problems they can't handle on their own. Unlike other Netherese cities, the courts here never close—there's simply too much work to do.

If player characters find themselves here, it's most likely due to one of two reasons. The first—and more pleasant—reason for visiting the Constable's is that they're looking for work. If that's the case, a gruff human

male points them toward another office filled with books that bears a brass plaque that reads "Bounty Office." Here, player-characters can get work—and earn rewards—by capturing some of Netheril's most wanted criminals. In addition, priests of Amaunator (or any other individual that can prove he is fair and impartial) can solve disputes for the courts, earning 100 gp per successful resolution.

The second reason for a trip to the Constables is because the player-characters have broken a law, such as robbing the bank or breaking into Nopheus's home. Characters are held in jail for no more than a day before they get their case heard in court.

Trials which resemble quick hearings decide the fate of the accused; justice is quick and mostly irreversible. Those accused of nonlethal crimes are generally sentenced to hard labor (typically 1–4 years for most offenses), while murderers are either sold into slavery to a visiting spelljamming vessel or executed within a day of sentencing.

C. Dock Hand Guild

Located right off of Helm Harbor, this guild serves the interest of the spelljamming community of Yeoman's Loft. The workers of this guild are well paid, but the work is hard and time consuming. The guildsmen are typically organized into groups of four men who use their minor magical abilities (cantras) to make their lives a little easier.

Visitors to the guild hall are given a cold stare by the workers gathered in the small (private) bar here. Adventurers who wander inside are approached by a member and asked their purpose in coming here. Money talks. This guild has little time or patience for charity.

The guild is a good source of rare alcohol from the depths of Realmspace. Spelljamming captains understand the need for keeping the dock workers happy, and many of them bring in cases of wine, ale, and mead from their journeys. For 500 gp or so, an interested party of adventurers can purchase such rare beverages.

D. Taverns

It's rare to go more than a few blocks in Yeoman's Loft without running into a tavern or two. The influx of traffic from spelljamming vessels frequently brings weary spacefarers into the city who are tired of being aboard ship. The farther away from the docks one gets, the more quiet the tavern.

There are two taverns quite popular in town. The first is the Spacer's Line, a rowdy establishment right off Helm Harbor. This is a favorite hangout for the more dangerous of the city's visitors. It's run by Eleron Mistif (CN hm F7), a retired spelljamming captain.

At the corner of Harbor Lane and Elm Street, the Captain's Fancy sits alone. It's a calm and restful tavern surrounded by a garden that serves only the finest drinks and food available. As the name implies, it's a favorite resting spot for spelljamming captains.

E. Hostels

These are simply single-person sleeping quarters for crewmen weary of life on board spelljamming vessels. The rooms are generally good quality, but no food or drink is provided. Most of the hostels provide a hot bath for a nominal fee of 1 silver piece. Rooms go for between 1 and 5 gold pieces a night.

F. Grocer Cartel

With the exception of the headquarters on Helm Road, all of the other buildings associated with the cartel are used solely for storing goods collected from the spelljamming traffic. The Grocer Cartel makes sure that all negotiations conducted for spelljamming goods are to the benefit of the city, but it's main goal is to prevent price wars that would be bad for business.

The guild is led by Ravenar Andarlis (LE hm T15), who also owns Andarlis Transport, one of the largest magical shipping companies in Netheril. He is a fair but unforgiving man who favors contracts (but only those agreements which are favorable to him). Many suspect that Ravenar is head of the thieves' guild of the Loft as well, but that's not the case. His brother, Silvin, is actually head of the guild.

G. Supply Vendors

These shops hold a variety of spare parts, raw materials, and other miscellaneous goods that the spelljamming vessels have come to expect. They're primarily warehouses that prefer dealing only with other businesses.

H. Bathhouses

The various bathhouses of the Loft are communal bathing pools for all manner of folk. Private baths are also popular, but a great deal of idle gossip and rumors also circulate through these structures, and the most common way folks learn what's happening is by listening to others talk about current events.

Silvin Lissender (LE hm T13) owns most of the bathhouses in town, and he also runs the thieves' guild from them. His real last name is Andarlis, but that's a secret only he and his brother, Ravenar, share.

No thievery occurs in the bathhouse—and it's a rule that Silvin enforces ruthlessly. More often than not, rich patrons have their belongings checked while they're taking a bath—then they're robbed at a more opportune time.

I. Courthouse/Jail

The courthouse is a magnificent structure that was obviously constructed with a great deal of magic. Huge slabs of marble form pillars that form an arc over the entrance. A golden luminescence surrounds the structure at night, providing an aura of light that serves as a beacon for the city's residents.

Within the halls are six huge court rooms that are always busy with cases (each of which take 1d4 hours to hear). Each court is administered by a sunlord or sunlady (priest of

Amaunator) of at least 12th level. As witnesses and the accused are brought forward, each is checked for magical emanations. Once purged of magic, each person involved in the trial is given a dose from a *potion of truth* (which acts like the ring of the same name and has a duration of 1d4 hours).

The jail is a bright and cheerful facility that is mostly empty during the day. Prisoners are taken to a mining camp a few miles outside of the city where they proceed to haul dirt, rocks, and other debris from nearby mines. At night, prisoners eat a hearty dinner and speak with a priest of Amaunator (or other court-appointed counselor) about the reasons they're in jail, what they did wrong, and similar topics.

J. Temple of Amaunator

Located a block away from the courthouse, the temple to Amaunator is nearly as large as the Loft's hall of justice. The temple serves not only as the headquarters for Amaunator's religion in the city, but as a school of law as well.

The temple is led by Sunlady Margaress (LN hf P13), an expert in Netherese and elven laws and procedures. She seldom participates in cases any more, however, preferring to teach in the temple.

K. Temple of Mystryl

This building is actually a small structure surrounded by a garden. Inside its stone walls is a small chamber consisting of around a dozen wooden pews and a raised stone dais upon which rests an altar.

The temple is run by the highest-level Dweomerkeeper who happens to be in the city at the time. This leads to a wide range of official "church policy" for the temple, but it also keeps the faithful apprised as to the activities elsewhere in Netheril.

L. Temple of Tyche

The most popular church in Yeoman's Loft, the Lady of Smiles is a favorite patron for those engaged in the dangerous business of transporting goods into Realmspace. Spacefarers likewise pay at least lip service to Lady Fate, reminding any who ask that a little luck can mean the difference between survival and disaster in the skies above Faerûn.

The temple is led by Kismetic Shantress Porstalle (CG hf P15). Shantress won a fortune in gold and platinum at a gambling den in Karsus five years ago, and she decided to settle down in the Loft and invest some of her wealth in Realmspace activities. She currently owns a small spelljamming vessel (40-ton) named *Lady Luck* that remains in Helm Harbor for her use.

M. Shipwrights

Each of these buildings is home to a different craftsman who specializes in the creation and repair of spelljamming vessels. The facilities in the Loft are capable of repairing only the more "human" spelljamming vessels (like hammerheads and wasps), and don't have the resources to repair elven vessels.

N. Oberon's Laboratory

This small, nondescript building is set apart from others on the block by a small wooden sign which reads: "Yeoman's Loft Historical Site—Oberon's Laboratory." A rickety set of steps lead up to a brass-bound wooden door that is always open during the day.

Upon entering, a visitor immediately realizes that the interior dimensions exceed those of the outside by a factor of at least two. On a pedestal at the entryway, a raised plaque reads:

Oberon (2839–2905) was the founder of Netheril's aerocosmology industry, the father of Realmspace. The son of a shipbuilder who grew up in Harborage, Oberon quickly put his magical skills into the creation of spelljamming vessels that sailed over Netheril. A powerful and respected arcanist, Oberon led the other archwizards of Netheril into the Skies Above.

This museum is dedicated to what survived of Oberon's work. The one-silver-piece fee for the tour goes to the upkeep and protection of Oberon's legacy.

—Yeoman's Loft Historical League

Tours begin every half hour, and there are always people wandering around the laboratory. Hundreds of items lie scattered around, protected under *walls of force* and stood watch over by around a dozen guards. These items range from small, hand-held accelerators (devices which hurl anything placed within them at tremendous speeds) to portable spelljamming helms (devices draped over the back that provided movement equivalent to a *fly* spell). All of the items in the museum are quasimagical prototypes, however, as Oberon didn't want to lay waste to his body as he experimented.

Despite all of the advances that Oberon was undoubtedly responsible for, there is no sign of a true spelljamming helm—the device needed to make a ship capable of travel through Realmspace. That particular invention was in the sole realm of the Arcane, who controlled the purchase of all spelljamming helms during the time of Netheril.

O. Spacefarers' Guild

Much like the dock hands' guild, the spacefarers' guild is composed of those who make their living by working on spelljamming vessels. They have little time for "tourists" to ask them questions about how a particular device works.

The guild does accept new members, but learning the craft of spelljamming is a time-consuming task. It takes more than a year to go through the course of studies offered at the guild, and initiates must pay a 500-gp fee for the schooling. The *Complete Spacefarers' Handbook* has a complete listing of proficiencies for DMs who incorporate spelljamming into their Netheril campaign.

P. Warehouses

These large buildings are primarily used as holding areas for the goods brought in from Helm Harbor. They're typically guarded by 2d6 guards at night and 3–6 guards during daylight hours.

Trek Through the Eastern Forest

uarded and sanctified, the wood hath delivered in labor the elf. Guardian and keeper, these souls, as everlasting as the woods of their birth, protect with their lives the lives of the wood.

Netheril may be known fondly as the greatest time of human existence, but all is not well with it. The Neth leaders are losing control of the wilderness. The phaerimm's incessant barrage of antimagic and life-leeching magic has caused much of the land to contort into a desert. The antimagic is nullifying the weather-controlling magic set up in the early years of Netheril, creating a growth in the northern glaciers (The High Ice) that has been held back for millennia. In recent years, the winters have been more severe.

With the loss of control over nature, the monsters are coming back. The orcs and the gnolls, once only a mere nuisance, were easily controlled and removed by the archwizards whenever the call for help from the surface cities arose. Now, however, the archwizard's ability to assist the groundling villages is severely limited, and the lower cities are suffering greatly. This is creating a disdain that cannot be curbed; a rift is growing between the flying enclaves and groundling civilization, and revolt seems to be on the horizon.

The Journey

With Nopheus's map in hand, the characters can set off to their destiny. As they travel through the mountains and the forest, the DM should roll for random encounters. Remember that parts of this adventure can be rather lethal, so the DM shouldn't rely on random encounters to weaken and tire the characters too much, otherwise no one will survive.

Random Encounters

Not every random encounter results in an armed attack against the player characters. Intelligent monsters normally try to determine the relative strength of a party before charging headlong into combat. Likewise, weaker creatures tend to run the moment it's clear that they are facing a superior foe.

Eastern Forest

Encounters in the Eastern Forest are checked once every four hours by rolling a 12-sided die; on a roll of 1 an encounter occurs. Roll a d20 and consult the Random Encounter table, then find the creature's listing below.

Ankhegs

Characters get their first warning of trouble when the lead character nearly falls into a large hole in the forest floor (successful Dexterity check to avoid). Within 1d4 rounds, the ankhegs arrive.

Ankhegs (1d6): AC 2/4 (underside); MV 12, Br 6; HD 5; hp 30 each; #AT 1; Dmg 3d6 (crush) + 1d4 (acid); SZ H (15' long); ML average (9); XP 600 each.
SA: Can squirt a stream of acid to a distance of 30 feet once every six hours. The acid causes 8d4 points of damage (half if a successful saving throw versus breath weapon is made).

Barbarians

These patrols are either barbarians providing their children a chance at entering adulthood (by defeating a chosen enemy, most likely orcs or goblins) or a patrol sent in to retaliate against orcs, kobolds, or goblins for a previous raid.

The barbarians are led by a 5th-level fighter; the remainder are 1st-level fighters. They're not dangerous to the party unless provoked, but their manner is somewhat distant.

Choke Creeper

Attentive characters have a 15% chance to notice that the particular trail they've been following is less traveled than others. Rangers can detect that no creatures have passed this way for at least three weeks (the orcs were smart enough to avoid this area after they lost a few hunting parties). If characters continue, they run across the choke creeper, which immediately attacks.

Choke Creeper (1): AC 6 (main vine)/5 (branches); MV ½; HD 25; hp 200; THAC0 7; #AT 64; Dmg 1d4; SZ G (160' long); ML elite (14); XP 18,000.
SA: 10% chance per round of strangling a struck creature. Strangled creatures die in one round. Immune to torch fire. Lightning attacks double movement for 1d4+1 rounds. Each vine that attacks has 16 hit points of its own.
SW: Suffers only 1 hp per die versus cold damage, but affected areas are stunned for 1d4+1 rounds.

Cloro, the Green Dragon

The trail the adventurers have been following begins to become very dense, blocking out the light from above. Soon, the party finds themselves walking through a tunnel of branches toward a clearing far ahead.

The last 120 feet of the tunnel is trapped every 10 feet with either a magical or mechanical device designed to warn Cloro of unexpected visitors in addition to delivering damage.

At the end of the tunnel stand two men clad in chain mail armor. The moment they see or hear the characters, one of them rushes off to inform Cloro that she has visitors. It's *very* unlikely that the party can sneak into Cloro's lair undetected.

When the party enters, the dragon confronts them at the exit to the tunnel, keeping as many people inside the tunnel as possible (that way she can get more of them with her breath weapon). She'll engage in some idol talk until someone makes a move to attack her, in which case she uses her breath weapon first as she orders her two *charmed* servants to attack.

Cloro, very old green dragon: AC –5; MV 9, Fl 30 (C), Sw 9; HD 18; hp 104; THAC0 3; #AT 3 + special; Dmg 1d8/1d8/2d10; MR 40%; SZ G (160' long); ML elite (16); XP 18,000.
SA: Can use her chlorine gas breath weapon that delivers 18d6+9 hit points of damage to all creatures in its area of effect, which is 50' long, 40' wide, and 30' high (a successful save vs. breath weapon reduces the damage to half). Casts all spells as if she was 15th level. Can cast *suggestion*, *water breathing* (at will), *warp wood* (three times a day), and *plant growth* once per day unless otherwise noted.
SD: Immune to all gases.
Spells (Dragon magic works normally and is not subject to the rules presented in the *Netheril: Empire of Magic* set): 1st Level: *charm person*, *magic missile*, *shield*, *shocking grasp*; 2nd Level: *mirror image*, *web*

Reliton and Gnarish, hm F3 (*charmed*): AC 5 (chain mail); MV 12; hp 22, 18; #AT 1; Dmg 1d8 (long sword); SZ M (6' tall); ML n/a; AL CG; XP 65 each.

Random Encounters

Eastern Forest	d20 Roll	Gods' Legion Mountains
2d4 orcs (Thousand Fists)	1	2d6 dwarves
1 choke creeper	2	2d10 ghouls and 1d4 ghasts
2d8 gnolls	3	5d4 Netherese merchants
5d4 orcs (Thousand Fists)	4	2d10 hobgoblins
1d6 wyverns	5	3d6 werewolves
9d6 orcs (Thousand Fists)	6	9d6 orcs (Rocktroll)
5d4 Netherese merchants	7	1 beholder
5d4 kobolds	8	1d4 mountain giants
2d10 large spiders	9	3d4 barbarians (Angardt)
6d6 Netherese fighters	10	1d4 manticores
2d10 ghouls and 1d4 ghasts	11	2d8 wights
6d6 orcs (Rocktroll)	12	6d6 orcs (Thousand Fists)
1d6 ankhegs	13	2d8 hippogriffs
2d4 owlbears	14	6d6 orcs (Thousand Fists)
1d4 ettins	15	2d10 hobgoblins
4d6 goblins	16	1d4 galeb duhr
6d4 elves (Cormanthyr)	17	1d10 stone giants
3d4 barbarians (Angardt)	18	5d4 orcs (Thousand Fists)
2d10 ogres	19	2d8 gnolls
1 very old green dragon (Cloro)	20	1 old red dragon (Pyrothraxis)

All of Cloro's treasure is in a small lake that is at the center of the clearing. About 60 feet down (buried under more than 23,000 copper pieces) are: 30,000 silver pieces, 16,000 gold pieces, 2,500 platinum pieces, 54 gems (use Table 85 in the DMG to determine value), a *mistress mask**, 3 *ioun stones*, a *rod of multiport**, a *ring of protection +3*, a *long sword +4 defender*, a *mace +3*, and 3 *potions of extra healing*. Items marked with an asterisk (*) are detailed in the *Encyclopedia Arcana* from the *Netheril: Empire of Magic* expansion set.

Elves

Each group of elves consists of warriors and mages (though the Netherese still call them arcanists). Each band is led by a 5th-level fighter/mage and also has at least two mages of 3rd level.

They're very interested in the activities of the orcs, kobolds, and goblins in the area. They are aware of the massive orc city in the Gods' Legion, but they explain that they're not ready to handle that problem just yet. After exchanging any information they might have with the party, they continue on their patrol.

Ettins

These giants have spotted the party from a nearby hill or clearing and are now moving to intercept the adventurers. They normally attack only at night, though they could have been disturbed by the heroes' trek through the wilderness.

Ettins (1d4): AC 3; MV 12; HD 10; THAC0 10; #AT 2; Dmg 1d10/2d6 (if disarmed) or 3d6/2d6 (spiked clubs); SZ H (13' tall); ML elite (14); XP 3,000 each.
SD: Surprised only on a roll of 1. *Infravision* to a range of 90 feet.

Each ettin is carrying 10d4 copper pieces and 10–30 silver. If the characters track the ettins back to their lair, they discover 2,014 silver pieces, 407 platinum pieces, and three gems (an amethyst worth 100 gp, a topaz worth 500 gp, and a fire opal worth 1,000 gp).

Ghouls & Ghasts

Silence isn't one of these creatures' finer points, and characters can hear them tramping through the forest from 100 yards away (though they won't actually see them until 30 yards or so).

Ghouls (2d10): AC 6; MV 9; HD 2; hp 10 each; THAC0 19; #AT 3; Dmg 1–3/1–3/1d6; SZ M (5–6' tall); ML steady (12); XP 175.
SA: Successful attack causes paralyzation in humans (except elves) for 3+1d6 rounds unless the target makes a successful saving throw versus paralyzation.
SD: Immune to *sleep* and *charm* spells.
SW: *Protection from evil* prevents a ghoul from attacking the protected creature.

Ghasts (1d4): AC 4; MV 15; HD 4; hp 23 each; THAC0 17; #AT 3; Dmg 1d4/1d4/1d8; SZ M (5–6' tall); ML elite (14); XP 650.
SA: Creatures within 10 feet must make a saving throw versus poison or fight with a –2 penalty. Successful attack causes paralyzation in humans (including elves) for 4+1d6 rounds unless the target makes a successful saving throw versus paralyzation.
SD: Immune to *sleep* and *charm* spells. Only a *protection from evil* spell cast with cold iron components can keep them at bay.
SW: Cold-wrought iron weapons inflict double damage.

The ghouls carry no treasure, but each ghast is carrying 5 gems of varying values. One of the ghasts has a *potion of sweetwater* in a small sack. If the party tracks the creatures back to their lair, they discover an additional 1,250 gold pieces, two small figurines of archwizards (each worth around 500 gp), and a *long sword +2*.

Gnoll Patrol

These creatures have a small cave complex they're guarding against orc incursion. While they don't particularly like the Netherese, they are more concerned about orcs in the area. Roughly half of any patrol is armed with polearms and missile weapons.

Gnolls (2d8): AC 5; MV 9; HD 2; hp 11 each; THAC0 19; #AT 1; Dmg 2d4 (broad sword), 1d10 (halberd), or 1d6 (short bow); SZ L (7 ½' tall); ML steady (11); XP 35 each.

Each gnoll carries 3d4 gems (all ornamental stones worth 10 gp each). The gnolls' treasure lies protected back at their camp, a community of 350 gnolls that is northeast of the current path the party is taking by one full day.

Goblins

The goblins guard "their" area of the forest jealously, attacking any and all intruders they encounter. This particular group is just a small patrol sent out from their village to make sure the elves, kobolds, orcs, or Netherese aren't planning an attack against them.

Each force of goblins attacks first by hurling their spears at the intruders. After that, goblins mounted on worgs charge in to attack, followed by the remainder of the force.

Goblins (4d6): AC 6; MV 6; HD 1–1; hp 5 each; THAC0 20; #AT 1; Dmg 1d6 (spear and mace); SZ S (4' tall); ML average (10); XP 15 each.

Worgs (6): AC 6; MV 18; HD 3+3; hp 20 each; THAC0 17; #AT 1; Dmg 2d4; SZ M (6' long); ML steady (11); XP 120.

Each goblin carries 3d6 silver pieces. Back at their village lies the bulk of their treasure, but such an endeavor would be an adventure of its own, the details of which are left to the DM.

Kobolds

The kobolds won't attack the adventurers unless they outnumber them at least two to one. They're much more concerned about the orcs and goblins in the area (though if the party has gnomes in it, the kobolds are 75% likely to attack, throwing everything they've got at the gnomes).

Kobolds (5d4): AC 7; MV 6; HD 1/2; HP 3 each; THAC0 20; #AT 1; Dmg 1d4 (claws) or 1d6 (weapons); SZ S (3' tall); ML average (9); XP 15 each.
SA: *Infravision* to 60 feet.
SW: Suffer –1 on attack rolls when in bright sunlight.

Each kobold carries 3d4 copper pieces and 1d4 silver pieces. Farther east into the forest is the home of these kobolds, a community some 300 strong.

Large Spiders

The path the players have been following slowly begins to fill with thick webs to either side of the trail. Characters with the observation proficiency can make a check with a –4 penalty to notice the webs; a ranger who makes a successful tracking check likewise detects the webs.

If the spiders' presence isn't detected, the lead character blunders into a thick web that has been set into the shadows. A character in the webs can escape in a number of rounds equal to his Strength score subtracted from 19 (character with 19 or greater Strength can walk right through the web). As soon as a character strikes the webs, the spiders leap out to attack.

Large Spiders (2d10): AC 8; MV 6, Wb 15; HD 1+1; hp 7 each; #AT 1; Dmg 1 + poison (type A); SZ S (2' diameter); ML unsteady (7); XP 175 each.
SA: Creatures stuck in a web are attacked with a +4 bonus and lose any benefit from a high Dexterity score.

Hidden nearby under a heavy blanket of webs is the treasure hoard of the spiders (actually whatever they couldn't eat off of their victims). There are 16 cp, 12 sp, 7 gp, and 11 pieces of electrum.

Netherese Fighters

A force of 6d6 warriors from the nearby cities are making a patrol of the "eastern shores of the Netheril Empire." They greet the PCs warmly, since they're the first signs of human life they've seen in many weeks. They talk to the PCs about one or two other encounters they've had in the last week (primarily orcs).

The force is led by Lord Grehnar (NG hm R9). The remainder of the warriors are between levels 2–4.

Netherese Merchants

A caravan of slow-moving merchants is slowly working its way up one of the trails. If approached by the player-characters, the caravan is very happy to see such "brave souls scouring the Eastern Forest of evil." They gladly equip the party with whatever nonmagical items they need and provide a hot meal to the heroes. The caravan is guarded by 50 warriors and arcanists of levels 1–3.

Ogres

These ogres hail from the massive orc city in the Gods' Legion Mountains. They've been sent out on their own to patrol, since they frequently get into altercations with the leaders of the various orc patrols.

Ogres (2d10): AC 5; MV 9; HD 4+1; hp 23 each; THAC0 17; #AT 1; Dmg 1d10 (fist) or 1d6+6 (clubs); SZ L (9' tall); ML steady (12); XP 270 each.
SA: Gain a +2 bonus on all attack rolls due to high Strength.

Each ogre is carry 2d4 gold pieces. The remainder of their treasure is back at the orc city (under the king's protection, of course).

Orcs (Thousand Fists)

These orcs are patrolling their homeland, keeping it safe from Netherese incursions and raiding parties from rival orc clans, goblins, kobolds, and other humanoids. They tend to attack on sight, retreating only when faced by powerful magic. Each group encountered always contains at least one shaman of 3rd level.

Orcs (any number): AC 6 (hide armor); MV 9; HD 1; hp 5 each; THAC0 19; #AT 1; Dmg 1d6 (short swords); SW –1 to attack and morale rolls while in sunlight; SZ M (6' tall); ML steady (11); Int avg (8); XP 15 each.

Orc shaman (1): AC 6 (hide armor); MV 9; HD 3; hp 17; THAC0 17; #AT 1; Dmg 1d6+1 (mace); SW –1 to attack and morale rolls while in sunlight; SZ M (6' tall); ML steady (11); Int avg (8); XP 175.
Winds available (4): Transcendent, sporadic, wandering. Favorite spells: *protection from good, hold person.*

Each orc is carry 1d4 pieces of electrum. The orcs' city is nestled against the slopes of the Gods' Legion Mountains and is home to 12,000 orcs.

Owlbears

These creatures rush out of the underbrush as the characters travel through the forest, gaining a +2 bonus on their ability to surprise. They do not retreat regardless of the actions of the party.

> **Owlbears (2d4):** AC 5; MV 12; HD 5+2; hp 33 each; THAC0 15; #AT 3; Dmg 1d6/1d6/2d6; SZ L (8' tall); ML n/a; XP 420 each.
> SA: On a roll of 18 or better, an owlbear drags its victim into a *hug*, inflicting 2d8 points of damage per round. The trapped creature is entitled to a single attempt at bend bars/lift gates to escape the hold.

Tracking the owlbears back to their lair is the only chance the adventurers have of obtaining any treasure off of them. Their lair is about three miles away from where the battle with the characters took place (successful tracking proficiency checks or similar abilities are required for each mile). Within the lair is 2,470 silver pieces, 210 platinum pieces, one magical item (DM's choice), and a quasimagical item (DM's choice).

Wyverns

As characters enter a light clearing in the forest, these creatures swoop down and attack. They're used to the orcs in the area, so it takes two failed Morale checks before they actually realize the danger they're in by a well-armed group of adventurers.

> **Wyverns (1d6):** AC 3; MV 6, Fl 24 (E); HD 7+7; hp 50 each; THAC0 13; #AT 2; Dmg 2d8/1d6; SZ G (35' long); ML very steady (14); XP 1,400 each.
> SA: Tail attack injects poison (type F) into the target upon a successful strike. Creatures must make a saving throw versus poison or die. Prefers to swoop down from the air and carry victims away (during which time it gains a +4 bonus to all attack rolls).

The wyverns don't carry any treasure on them; their nest is many miles away (and since the player's can't track flying creatures, there is little chance they can find it). If they do manage to track it down somehow, its contents are left to the discretion of the Dungeon Master.

Gods' Legion Mountains

Encounters in the mountains are checked once every four hours by rolling an 8-sided die; on a roll of 1 an encounter occurs. Roll a d20 and consult the Random Encounter table, then find the creature's listing below.

Barbarians (Angardt)

This group of barbarians is just making a sweep of the mountains to try and find a band of orcs that raided a barbarian encampment a few days ago. They're not aware of the huge orc city at the northern end of the mountains and will be quite surprised to learn that the orcs exist in such large numbers (they thought they eliminated the orc threat years ago).

Beholder

Just as the party is climbing a slight embankment, this awesome creature floats into view, letting out a roar. Moments earlier, it thought it heard something outside its cave. The players just happened to be in the wrong place at the wrong time.

> **Beholder (1):** AC 0 (body)/2 (eyestalk)/7 (eyes); MV Fl 3 (B); HD 70 hit points; THAC0 5; #AT 1; Dmg 2d4; SZ M (6' in diameter); ML fanatic (18); Int exceptional (16); XP 14,000.
> SA: Eyestalks can fire magical spells; *charm person, charm monster, sleep, telekinesis, flesh to stone, disintegrate, fear, slow,* and *cause serious wounds.*
> SD: Central eye projects an area of anti-magic to a distance of 140 yards in a 90 degree arc in front of it.

Within the lair are seven gems (determine value randomly by using Table 85 in the DMG) and five works of art (Table 87 in the DMG). There are also a variety of lifelike statues in the chamber, one of which is an artist who claims that the pieces of art were his before he was ambushed by the beholder (assuming the characters try a *flesh to stone* spell on the "lifelike statue"). He grudgingly gives them up if the party seems affronted, since they did rescue him, after all.

Dwarves

From time to time, the dwarves of Delzoun sent out groups in an attempt to establish trade with the various elven nations in the area. This is one of those groups, returning home somewhat dour from their latest failure. The dwarves are all 1st to 3rd level and not in the most talkative of moods.

Galeb Duhr

The party is alerted to the sounds of danger ahead by the sounds of a boulder crashing into the ground. As they round a bend, they notice an orc slowly disappearing into a pool of mud. Within moments, the scene is peaceful.

The galeb duhr don't desire contact with the party. So long as the party doesn't make an extensive search of the area, the galeb duhr ignore their presence.

> Galeb Duhr (1d4): AC –2; MV 6; HD 10; hp 73, 67, 64, 60; THAC0 11; #AT 2; Dmg 4d6/4d6; MR 20%; SZ L (12' tall); ML fanatic (17); Int very (12); XP 10,000 each.
> SA: Can cast *move earth, stone shape, passwall, transmute rock to mud,* and *wall of stone* once per day at 20th-level of ability. They can cast *stone shape* at will. They can animate 1–2 boulders around them.
> SD: Gain +4 versus fire-based attacks.
> SW: Suffer a –4 penalty to saving throws versus cold, in addition to suffering double damage from cold-based attacks.

Beneath a nearby rock are 3d4 gems and two potions (*extra healing* and *fire resistance*).

Ghouls & Ghasts

A priest of Jergal came across this group of ghouls late at night and decided to take control of them and order them about. They were performing various chores for the old priest when Jergal finally came to claim him—in the form of ghasts that feasted upon his body. The group is wild and uncontrolled now, searching out new victims. Their statistics and treasure are identical to the **Ghouls & Ghasts** entry under the Forest Encounters.

Gnolls

These are identical to the gnolls listed in the Eastern Forest section.

Hippogriffs

These creatures are out looking for orcs that raided their nest, killing one of their young in the process. The moment they see the party, they take them to be their enemies and attack.

Hippogriffs (2d8): AC 5; MV 18, Fl 36 (C, D); HD 3+3; hp 20 each; THAC0 17; #AT 3; Dmg 1d6/1d6/1d10; SZ L (10' long); ML average (9); Int semi (2); XP 175 each.

Back at their nest is the remainder of their treasure; 3d4 gems (refer to Table 85 in the DMG for values).

Hobgoblins

This force of hobgoblins is scouting the trails for orcs, goblins, and kobolds who are infringing on the hobgoblins' territory. They more than happily attack anything they think they can dominate, as they try to demonstrate to the heroes the moment they catch sight of them (concentrating their initial volley of missile attacks against elves).

Hobgoblins (2d10): AC 5; MV 9; HD 1+1; hp 7 each; THAC0 19; #AT 1 (melee) or 2 (missile); Dmg 1d8 (long sword) or 1d6 (short bows with flight arrows); SZ M (6 ½' tall); ML steady (11); XP 35 each.

Each hobgoblin carries 3d8 copper pieces and 2d4 gold pieces. Their weapons are well cared for, however.

Manticores

These fierce creatures fly into view, scattering small rocks and twigs as they land nearby to attack. They always release a volley of tail spikes as their first attack and then close with their prey.

Manticores (1d4): AC 4; MV 12, Fl 18 (E); HD 6+3; hp 48, 42, 37, 33; THAC0 13; #AT 3; Dmg 1–3/1–3/1d8; SZ H (15'); ML elite (13); Int low (5); XP 975 each.

Mountain Giants

As the party is traversing a path, these giants suddenly stand at the edge of a nearby cliff and begin tossing boulders at them. Each giant is far enough away from the other so that area of effect spells like *Noanar's fireball* can't get them both.

Mountain Giants (1d4): AC 4; MV 12; HD 15+3; hp 115, 107, 99, 92; THAC0 5; #AT 1; Dmg 2d10 (boulders) or 4d10+10 (clubs); SZ H (14' tall); ML champion (15); Int average (9); XP 7,000.
SA: Can summon other creatures, but this takes a full turn to perform and requires a wait of 1d6 hours before the summoned creatures arrive.
SW: Strong stench reveals their presence for hundreds of feet downwind.

The mountain giants are not carrying any treasure. Their lair is a large cave a few miles away from the ambush.

Netherese Merchants

These fortune seekers believe that there is a vast wealth to be made in these mountains by opening up trade with gnomes, renegade halflings, a new dwarven kingdom, and the giants. Unfortunately, they haven't been able to find anything except for the giants (who have attacked them each time they've met).

They're led by Danvren Goodsale, a human merchant from Yeoman's Loft. He's absolutely convinced that these other "lost tribes" exist out here, but they've decided to return back to Yeoman's Loft and resupply before venturing out once again.

There are around 30 guards and 20 merchants remaining in the caravan, and virtually all of them are in need of healing. Danvren agrees to pay the party 1,000 gold pieces if they escort them back to Yeoman's Loft (he can't afford to lose any more men or wagons to the monsters).

Orcs (Rocktroll)

The actual Rocktroll orcs reside toward the southern end of the Gods' Legion Mountains, but they frequently send out groups to watch the movements of the Thousand Fists orcs and to make sure armies are not gathering to attack their own city. There is a 75% chance that these orcs attack the party; on a roll of 76% or higher, they ignore the heroes.

Orcs (any number): AC 6 (hide armor); MV 9; HD 1; hp 5 each; THAC0 19; #AT 1; Dmg 1d6 (short swords); SW –1 to attack and morale rolls while in sunlight; SZ M (6' tall); ML steady (11); Int avg (8); XP 15 each.

Each orc is carry 2d6 pieces of electrum.

Orcs (Thousand Fists)

These orcs are simply out patrolling their homeland, attacking any creature they think they can defeat. At the first sign of trouble, however, at least one of the orcs runs back to the city to report the party's presence.

Orcs (any number): AC 6 (hide armor); MV 9; HD 1; hp 5 each; THAC0 19; #AT 1; Dmg 1d6 (short swords); SW –1 to attack and morale rolls while in sunlight; SZ M (6' tall); ML steady (11); Int avg (8); XP 15 each.

Each orc is carrying 2d6 pieces of platinum.

Pyrothraxis, Red Dragon

The trees in this area are mostly burned stumps, and the lip of a long-extinct volcano can be seen in the distance. Looking down into the volcano, the party sees the sprawling lair of Pyrothraxis, an old red dragon.

The only way into the lair is by climbing or through use of magic; there are no side tunnels that lead into the area. Pyrothraxis is lightly dozing near a large pile of gems and gold pieces (and will awaken the moment anyone begins climbing down or starts casting a spell).

Pyrothraxis, old red dragon: AC –7; MV 9, Fl 30 (C), Jp 3; HD 19; hp 132; THAC0 1; #AT 3; Dmg 1d10/1d10/3d10; MR 45%; SZ G (130'); ML fanatic (18); Int exceptional (16); XP 19,000.

SA: A cone of fire breath weapon that is 90' long and 30' wide at the end that inflicts 16d10+8 (saving throw versus breath weapon for half) points of damage. Can *affect normal fires* (3 times/day), *pyrotechnics* (3 times/day), *heat metal* and *suggestion* (both once/day).

SD: Immune to fire.

Spells: 1st Level: *magic missile, shocking grasp*. 2nd Level: *Melf's acid arrow, web*; 3rd level: *lightning bolt*.

A favored tactic of Pyrothraxis is to wait for creatures to begin scaling the side of the volcano and then *web* them into place. Once the creatures have been webbed, they automatically fail their saving throw versus his breath weapon.

Despite the fact that dragons aren't subjected to the Netherese spellcasting system, their spells still inflict damage without a cap. For example, Pyrothraxis's *lightning bolt* inflicts 19d6 points of damage.

The precise treasure of Pyrothraxis's lair is left to the DM, but it should be considerable. If the party chooses to take on this old dragon, it should be a fight that costs a few of them their lives (if not the entire party).

Stone Giants

These giants are standing motionless among the rocks as they watch the party pass. Elves have a 1-in-6 chance (a roll of 1 on a d6) to notice the giants watching them. The giants do nothing unless the party begins to move toward their cave a few hundred yards away.

Stone Giants (1d10): AC 0; MV 12; HD 14 + 1–3 hit points; hp 95 each; THAC0 7; #AT 1; Dmg 3d10 (boulders) or 2d6+8 (giant clubs); SZ H (18' tall); ML champion (16); Int average (9); XP 7,000 each.

If the party begins moving toward the cave, the stone giants first cause an avalanche, which inflicts 4d10 points of damage against all creatures in its area of effect (120 feet long at the base). All of the giants' treasure is stored in the cave (where another 20 stone giants await).

Werewolves

If this encounter is rolled during the day, wait until the second watch is half-completed that night before the werewolves attack. The werewolves charge into camp and attack for four rounds, retreating if they haven't totally dominated their targets. Depending on their success, they trail the party and attack each night.

Werewolves (3d6): AC 5; MV 15; HD 4+3; hp 23 each; THAC0 15; #AT 1; Dmg 2d4; SZ M (6' tall); ML steady (12); XP 420 each.

SA: Damage caused by a successful attack has a chance to inflict *lycanthrope* on the victim (1% per point of damage caused; check at the end of the encounter).

SD: Can be harmed only by silver or magical weapons.

Wights

From what appears to be the site of an avalanche, these undead emerge and immediately charge at any living creature in the area, picking elves and other nonhumans over humans when possible. The wights appear to have once been orcs.

Wights (2d8): AC 5; MV 12; HD 4+4; hp 28 each; THAC0 15; #AT 1; Dmg 1d4 + 1-level energy drain; SZ M (5' tall); ML elite (14); Int average (9); XP 1,400 each.

SD: Can be struck only by silver or +1 or better magical weapons. Immune to sleep, charm, hold, paralyzation, poison, and cold-based attacks.

SW: Holy water inflicts 2d4 points of damage. A *raise dead* spell totally destroys a wight.

The wights have managed to gather a decent horde of treasure since their death many years ago. Beneath the rubble is: 3,500 copper pieces, 600 platinum pieces, 6 gems (use Table 85 in the DMG to determine value), a suit of *chain mail +2*, and a *long bow, +1*.

Planned Encounters

During their trek, there are five planned encounters that occur. **The Summons** occurs first, with the remainder taking place as the DM deems appropriate.

The Summons

Just as the PCs begin their journey, they are met by a group of arcanists along the trail. There are no tracks anywhere around the three individuals save on the path itself, seeming to indicate that they used magic to arrive.

"Ah, right on time," smiles an older man in red robes that have a flaring "K" embroidered upon them. "Karsus does reward those who are prompt and faithful to Netheril." The old man bows low.

"I bring you greetings from the great Archwizard, Karsus himself. He desires your services in tracking down a few elusive spell components. Are you interested?"

If the characters say they're interested, the old arcanist states that his name is Jaston Willonay, Third Arcanist of Netheril—an honorary titled bestowed by Karsus. He goes on to explain that Karsus has need of such experienced adventurers.

"Karsus has need of two materials to prepare spell components. The first is the pituitary gland of the Tarrasque. The second is the stone-filled gizzard of a gold dragon." Jaston stops and studies your faces for a long moment.

"Some of you might have reservations about slaying a gold dragon just to get its gizzard for a spell component. I don't blame you. But I'm not here to compare ethics; all I can tell you is that these components are vital to the survival of Netheril.

"The gold dragon Dracolnobalen can be found in the northern reaches of Moander's Footstep. To the west of here in the Flats is the lair of the Tarrasque."

Jaston doesn't offer payment immediately; it's widely known throughout Netheril that Karsus is a man whose generosity has its own rewards. If the characters request any magical or quasimagical item in exchange for their services, Jaston accepts their terms. Likewise, if they request a reasonable sum of money, he also accepts.

If the player-characters try to extract an archwizard's ransom in exchange for the spell components, Jaston declines. He states that other adventuring parties have been sent on similar missions, and the party's assistance—while desired—isn't worth the price.

If the characters accept, they can continue their trek through the Eastern Forest, into the Gods' Legion Mountains, and finally to the base of Moander's Footstep. Once there, proceed to **The Search** on page 33.

It's important that the characters complete the first part of their quest (obtaining the spell components) before going after Nopheus's wife. If the party strays, Jaston reappears once or twice to urge them toward the gold dragon. If the characters are intent on rescuing Amanda first, then Jaston departs (and another adventuring party obtains the necessary components).

Varied Tracks

The party discovers humanoid tracks (dragged boots, bare feet, and evening slippers) heading east through the snow. More than 20 tracks can be seen, but if a ranger is in the group, he is able to determine that exactly 46 humanoids passed through the area sometime between two and five days previous.

☞ If the characters decide to follow the tracks, proceed to **The Graveyard** on page 22.

Frozen Bounty

A frozen skeleton, mostly flayed of its meat, reclines against an ice-covered evergreen, though fragmented breeches still cling to his naked hip bones. Rotted clothing (a coat, a scattered backpack, and a brown, wide-brim hat bearing the symbol of a snake entwining a scepter of gold) is also scattered around the snow.

Inside the backpack is a crumbled menu of items the deceased wished to purchase at the next city, a sevenday ration pack (partially consumed and showing the scrapings of small carnivorous teeth), a scroll tube (labeled "For Karsus's Eyes Only") sealed in wax and kissed with the mark of a signet ring, three folded and unused waterskins, and a small diary.

The ration pack is safe to eat, in spite of the teeth marks. The scroll tube is easily opened, having no protective magic and contains a small map detailing a path to a stash of hidden *nether scrolls* in western Netheril. If the characters follow the path outlined on the map, proceed to **Nether Here Nor There** on page 37.

The diary contains a variety of letters, characters, and symbols that don't make any sense whatsoever. It's actually protected by a *Raliteff's illusion script* spell, which allows only arcanists from the Karsus Enclave to read it. Other creatures making the attempt must make a saving throw versus spell or be affected by a *suggestion* spell that causes them to believe that the book is filled with the last few days of life for the skeleton (and rather boring at that). The diary is actually a journal of the movements of the Neth Underground for Freedom as well as a chronicle of the wrongs inflicted onto the people by the reigning archwizards.

☞ If the characters decide to bring the writings to the authorities on the Karsus Enclave, proceed to **Quelling the Serfs** on page 37.

☞ If the characters read the diary and decide to join the ranks of the freedom fighters, proceed to the **Liberty on my Mind** side trek on page 36.

Sound of Glory

Just before the party is ready to camp for the evening, they hear loud voices and the clamor of metal against metal from about 1,000 yards ahead. If the characters decide to investigate the din, start a fire, or otherwise draw attention to themselves, proceed to **A Thousand Fists Knocking** on page 31.

Elven Proposal

The PCs run into a group of elves who greet the characters as though they were longtime allies. They invite the heroes to share their fire with them for an evening of story-telling, merriment, and safety. The elven group consists of three rangers, 12 arcanists, four priests of various elven faiths, and six thieves.

The evening starts out with the elves sharing stories with the characters. Eventually, the elves bring out some fine wine and begin playing games, challenging one or two of the heroes to a game of chance (*creyala*, a form of elven poker using cards) or skill (such as darts). Slowly, the elves begin to try and pry the loyalties from the characters, deciding whether or not they are loyal to Karsus and the other archwizards.

If the elves find out that the characters are not of Netherese origin (time travelers) or that they hold no love for Karsus and the archwizards, they invite them into a business proposition. The elves immediately stop their merriment and get down to discussing the fine points of their deal with the heroes. Proceed to the **Thief in the Night** side trek on page 27.

If the characters are loyal to Karsus (or at least perceived to be), the elves still provide a night of fun and merriment. When morning dawns, they bid farewell to the heroes and then continue on their way.

The Graveyard

DM Note: The players should have retrieved the spell components for Karsus by this time, or else have been warned by Jaston that they are delaying the Archwizard's progress.

Hundreds of years ago, a shaman declared this grove of trees "by the voices of gods in his head" to be a holy place, and he cast a variety of spells across the area in an effort to shield it from necromantic magic. The area is surrounded by four soft, rolling hills, each being halfway between the points of a compass rose. In the center of the valley created by the hills, a huge shadowtop tree (probably as old as the forest or even the world itself) sits in supreme dignity; hundreds of animals make their homes in its branches in complete impunity.

For centuries, the elves of Shadowtop have used this special and holy area to bury their dead. Since the original consecration, many elves have been buried here, their lichen-covered driftwood or stone grave markers telling the tale of their tragic deaths.

The burial site, some 300-feet in diameter, is surrounded by a grove of Shadowtop trees so thick that walking two-abreast isn't possible. Weaving and writhing branches, fern growth, sun-starved underbrush, and oddly placed grave markers make travel extremely difficult.

Arrival

As the characters pass into the grave site, they behold a sorrowful sight: piles of dirt next to every tomb marker. Each of the graves have been unearthed, and some appear to have been excavated not from the outside, but from within. Nothing remains in the graves, not even small personal items that would be of no value.

As the characters investigate the area, they suddenly hear footsteps all around them. Appearing out of trees, dozens of elves surround the characters. As more elves appear, one says, "See. I reported the truth. Someone has raised our ancestors to perform malicious deeds. Perhaps it was these humans," he says, pointing at the party.

The elf suddenly marches stiff-legged and angry toward [lead human character], reaching up and reddening [his/her] left cheek with a well-placed backhand slap. The elf is immediately set upon by the other elves before anyone can react, who tackle him to the ground. There is a lot of arguing and shouting—all of it in elven—as the elves restrain one of their own.

An elf wearing *elven chain mail* and a purple cloak utters a word and suddenly all of the bickering stops. Obviously the leader of the elves, he speaks in common.

"Humans, as a whole, are our ancestral allies. Until we know otherwise, they're to be treated with respect and dignity." The leader pulls a dagger out of a scabbard and hands it—hilt forward—to [lead human character], saying, "It's our custom to slay one who has wronged us intentionally. This is now your right. His life is yours if you choose to take it."

If the character kills the elf, he does so with the first blow and nothing more is said of the matter. If the PC chooses not to kill his attacker, the elf is in the PC's debt for life.

If the PCs investigate the area, they discover a great number of tracks heading off in two separate paths toward the east. If they do not investigate, an elven ranger searches for tracks instead, finding the same results.

The leader of the Shadowtop Clan, Solocrian, suggests the characters take one path while a group of his finest warriors take the other, that way both avenues can be explored simultaneously. Regardless of the path the characters take, the results detailed below apply.

On the Trail of the Dead

The path heads east deep into the Eastern Forest. It winds over sharp hills, around steep cliffs, and through deep brush

and rivers. Occasionally, the path is joined by additional footsteps that merge with the current tracks, strengthening the path and making it easier and easier to follow.

The path carries the characters through areas where the ground has been dug up to expose a rotted wooden crate large enough to hold an average-sized human. No possessions remain, except the moldering remains of an elven death shroud.

As characters follow the trail of footsteps deeper into the forest, they begin to notice an abnormal number of flies in the area feasting upon what appears to be hunks of old, rotted meat. As evening approaches, characters come across the following:

> The decomposing body of an elf lies sprawled out on the trail. Its right leg is severed and more than a dozen teeth lie scattered around it. As you approach within 20 feet, the remains push themselves upright and the elf turns its head to face you with one empty eye socket. A smile seems to crease its way across the decaying skin.
>
> "I cannot go any farther, and my companions have left me behind to rot. You see, I seem to have broken my leg." He looks down at his lower limb which resembles an inch-think branch snapped across a knee; few sinews of meat remain. "Can you help me?"

Just about anything can aid the undead: a bit of *sovereign glue* to join the break, a nearby stick and a length of rope to bind the disjointed piece with the rest of the body, or a carefully placed *Aksa's repair* spell. Regardless of method, if the characters help the zombie, it shows its gratitude by standing, thanking the characters, and walking away—in the direction of its companions. (If allowed to rejoin the ranks of the dead, the zombie, Derf, warns all the others not to attack the characters and to consider them 'friend.')

If the characters attack, they gain a +4 bonus to attack and the zombie suffers a –4 penalty (prone). It's an easy kill, even for low-level characters, and the zombie cries out "No, no, it's not my fault," for the duration of the combat.

After a few days' travel, the characters approach a small village. The tracks pass through the main avenue, leading them directly into town. The town is deathly quiet; unusual for a frontier village. Most of the doors are open, but the windows are battened down. The street, showing the path of the undead, tells a horrifying tale.

In this town, the undead apparently entered every building and pulled the inhabitants from the ranks of the living to that of the dead, strengthening their numbers and taking the new recruits with them.

As the party searches around the town (or tries to leave), they are confronted by a berserk ranger who comes at them in a fever of hatred and fear, wildly wielding an axe head polearm glinting the rays of the cold afternoon sun. He screams something about wanting "the skulls of the dead" and then advances menacingly toward the heroes.

Anything can happen here. If the characters keep their distance and try to negotiate their way from this predicament, a flickering of sanity begins to fill the man's wild eyes. If they unsheathe their weapons and attack, his rage takes control and he attempts to kill everyone.

Anointus, hm, R15: AC –3; MV 12; hp 118; THAC0 6; #AT 2; Dmg 1d8/1d8 (polearm); MR 15% (from armor); SZ M (6 ½' tall); ML fearless (19); AL NG; XP 8,000.

Str 22, Dex 15, Con 18, Int 18/3, Wis 15, Cha 17.

Special Equipment: Separator (polearm), *Deflector* (shield), and *Protector* (armor). These belongings are detailed in the **Spells & Magic** chapter.

Spells (16/3rd): Anointus worships Selûne and gains access to the terrestrial and wandering winds.

Anointus, a ranger of some repute, is best known as a knowledgeable guide through the Wildlands of the Neth Southeast. He had family and friends who lived in this town. The loss of his wife and child, along with an unnatural increase in Strength and Constitution, has partially snapped his mind, explaining the two Intelligence ratings. When he's faced with undead, his Intelligence drops to the lower rating, but in situations away from undead, his Intelligence returns to normal.

Anointus looks almost prissy in both attire and appearance. His blonde hair is perfectly cut, combed, and styled, and his teeth are as pearly as the brightest cloud. His boots are spit-shined at least once a day, and all of his gear is meticulously cleaned, oiled, and sharpened (if applicable) every time it's pulled from its scabbard or used. After combat, he can typically be found sitting on the nearest rock or stump, cleaning his gear and resharpening his blades.

If the characters manage to calm Anointus when they first meet him, he tells them the following:

> I was commissioned by seven merchants from Spiel who wanted to enjoy the life of their ancestors: hunting, fishing, sleeping out of doors—all without the use of magic. This in itself wasn't unusual—I've taken many out into the wilds to rough it for a while—but traveling without magic was an unusual request.
>
> "I was amazed. Usually I have to hire a spellcaster who takes half my profits, but this time, each of their 2,000 gp charges went directly to me. We set out five days ago into the Eastern Forest with backpacks, waterskins, crossbows and bows, arrows and bolts, and enough flint for a year.
>
> A few days into the trip, we heard a horrid crashing through the trees. At first I thought it was either a lazy and vastly overpopulated orc patrol whose confidence overstepped all manner of prudence or the migration of a rhea herd moving toward better water and available food. In either case, I didn't want to be in the way, so we climbed trees and silently waited for the noise to dissipate. Imagine my surprise when I found a migration of undead passing directly under my tree!
>
> "I fought the urge to attack them on sight, especially when their numbers just kept coming. Hundreds of them, or even thousands. They were as thick as grass, practically touching each other as they went, darkening the ground below them. I looked over at the merchants who were ashen. I decided it was time to head back to town and see if they left the town unscathed.

"Apparently when the zombies entered the town, then whisked everyone away with them. The tracks lead to every building, and in each building signs of struggle is apparent. It looks like the undead just killed everyone in town, turned them into additional undead, and brought them along on their journey." Tears well up in Anointus's eyes, a glimmer of rage and sorrow reflected in them. "Most undead aren't that bright, so these must either be in the control of a god or an archwizard—but no archwizard that I know of would dare such an attack on innocents."

Anointus declines any offer to join the heroes, explaining that he works better alone and that he has some things he needs to check on—and he can't do it with a bunch of noisy greenhorns trailing along behind him. He's friendly about his reasons, but he can't be convinced to change his mind. He promises that he'll see them later, probably closer to whatever final destination the undead have in mind.

The Orc Retreat

The characters hear a great thrashing through the bushes ahead of them. Squeals of fear and grunting of hard labor are discernible as well. Within two minutes, a group of 30 orcs pass through the area where the characters are. If the

PCs are in the open, the orcs attempt to run around them in their panic. If the characters attempt to kill the orcs, they dodge and parry whatever blows they can in order to continue their flight.

If the characters capture one of the orcs, he's willing to talk in order to continue his retreat:

"Haven't you all heard? The Lichlord, Master of the Undead, Murderer of the Masses, Dread of the Archwizards, and Terror of the Earth, is amassing an army of the unliving in order to kill and take over everything! He believes that only the undead will treat the world with respect and discontinue the misuse of the environment. This means the extermination of all orcs, humans, gnomes, dwarves, and even those vile and irritating wood-huggers—you know, the elves.

"We've chosen life, and we're trying to get to our homelands in order to move our families and friends to the holy lands in the Spine of the World. He's amassing an army of dead so vast, it can crush any army it comes in contact with. It feeds on the war dead, making itself stronger as it moves west. Nothing can compete with that. If I were you, I'd turn my back on the east and join us in flight."

If the orc is asked where the Lichlord can be found, the orc points due east and replies, "The Lichlord is that way

about three days' travel. But be forewarned, the Omniscient One knows you approach and is prepared. Flee while you can and turn west. This is the only way you can save what life you have. He'll take it from you and give you the mindless euphoria of the living death if you continue your journey." After speaking with the characters, the orc wrestles free of their grasp and continues on his way.

The Elusive Illithid

Hungry for magic and seeking revenge, the phaerimm (detailed fully in the *Netheril: Empire of Magic* boxed set) have laid a shaky foundation of peace with the illithids. The pact between these two races is essentially a sharing of "resources." The phaerimm turn over all humans and humanoids they capture to the illithids, and the illithids probe the minds of the humans for any useful information.

If the characters and their companions are carrying any magical items, the phaerimm are able to detect their presence. Once they discover the characters, the phaerimm follow them (while remaining underground and out of phase in order to reduce their chance of discovery) and wait until nighttime when humanoids—in their experience—are less active.

Phaerimm (1–3): AC 1; MV Fl 9 (A); HD 9; hp 63; THAC0 11; #AT 6; Dmg 1d4×4/3d4/2d4; MR 44%/77% vs. polymorph and petrification; SZ L (12' tall); ML fanatic (17); Int supra (19); AL NE; XP 10,000.

SA— If the tail attack roll is 16 or better, the victim takes usual damage plus 1d6 more as the sting injects a fluid. The victim saves vs. poison three times: for *paralyzation*, to determine if victim is *levitated* three feet off the ground, and to see if a fertile egg is injected. If so, it begins growing in 1d6 days, internally eating the victim for one hit point per day until death or a *cure disease* is cast. Meanwhile, victim attacks, AC, and statistics are penalized four points. An egg or larva can be cut from a victim, requiring a System Shock and 2d4 damage during the process.

SD—160-foot *infravision* also sees in astral and ethereal planes 90', normal vision functions as *detect magic* for 90', reflect resisted spells back at source or use them as healing (excess points are carried for 12 rounds to offset later damage) while spells doing no damage heal one hit point per spell level.

Spells: (200/10th): These phaerimm cast spells as a 22nd-level arcanist (spells are at the DM's discretion).

If the phaerimm subdue one or more of the characters, they take the bodies with them to their allies, the illithids, in the depths of the earth (using planar travel spells to move into either the astral or ethereal planes).

Illithid (Mind Flayer) (4): AC 5; MV 12; HD 8+4; hp 61; THAC0 11; #AT 4; Dmg 2; MR 90%; SZ M (6' tall); ML champion (15); Int genius (18); AL LE; XP 9,000.

SA: Mind blast is a cone 60' long, 5' wide at the illithid, and 20' wide at the opposite end; all within the cone must save vs. wands or be stunned and unable to act for 3d4 rounds. Can cast the following spells as a 7th-level spellcaster: *suggestion, charm person, charm monster, ESP, levitate, astral projection,* and *plane shift*; all saving throws against these are made with a –4 penalty.

Psionic Summary (Only if used in the campaign): Level 10; Dis 4; Sci 5; Dev 15; Att EW, II; Def all; Score=18; PSPs 314, 307, 300, 284.

Psychokinesis Devotions: control body, levitation.

Psychometabolism Sciences: body equilibrium.

Psycoportation Sciences: probability travel, teleport.

Psychoportation Devotions: astral travel.

Telepathy Sciences: domination, mindlink.

Telepathy Devotions: contact, ESP, ego whip, id insinuation, posthypnotic suggestion.

The illithids, being creatures of great brain and psionic power, delve into their victims' minds and extract any useful information they can find. Once all information about Netheril and humans in general is extracted, the illithids eat the empty, wanting brains or feed the awake but unconscious character to their pets and watchdogs, the intellect devourers.

Intellect Devourer (2): AC 4; MV 15; HD 6+6; hp 48 each; THAC0 13; #AT 4; Dmg 1d4/1d4/1d4/1d4; SA Psionics, stalking; SD; MR Nil; SZ T (6" long); ML Fanatic (17–18); Int Very (11–12); AL CE; XP 6,000.

SA—Each successful hit causes an additional 1d4 points of damage unless the creature makes a successful saving throw versus poison.

SD—+3 or better weapon to hit (even then, the devourer only suffers 1 hit point of damage), immune to cerebral parasites and all mental attacks except psionic blast; immune to normal or magical fire; electrical attacks cause only 1 hit point per die of damage.

Psionic Summary: Level 6; Dis 3; Sci 3; Dev 11; Att EW, II; Def M-, TS, IF; Score=Int; PSPs 200.

Psychometabolism Sciences: ectoplasmic form.

Psychometabolism Devotions: body equilibrium, chameleon power, expansion, reduction.

Psychoportation Devotions: astral projection.

Telepathy Sciences: domination, mindlink.

Telepathy Devotions: aversion, contact, ESP, ego whip, id insinuation, telempathic projection.

While it's possible that characters could somehow escape the illithids, such an adventure is left to the DM. If the players managed to survive the encounter with the phaerimm, continue with **Dead Denizens** (page 43).

SIDE TREKS

eace is the way of the wise man, but is war always the path of the imprudent? Belief in the lie that one is the only justifiable ruler of a people is often the path of the folly, and the lie blinds him.

Throughout the adventure, there are several points where the Dungeon Master can send the characters on a little side quest. These are all listed here. The DM can choose to thread these throughout the adventure at the appropriate time, or he can simply use them as separate adventures. A rough experience point total is provided.

Side Trek Name	XP Totals
Thief In the Night	10,000
A Thousand Fists Knocking	15,335
Breaking and Entering	825–2,050
In Jail	13,000
The Search	138,000
Karsus Marketplace	—
Liberty On My Mind	12,025–16,985
Nether Here Nor There	—
Quelling the Serfs	66,840
Robin Banks	960
Scrying the Orcs Through	5,380+

tion about the protective magic therein. The elves claim that archived information about ultrahigh spellcasting is contained in this repository, while the Karsus Museum holds valuable magical items and recipes for elixirs that can grant just about anything one would wish.

If the characters take the map and attempt to infiltrate the repository on Delia, they must first get to the city.

Delia is a large city that houses between 375,000 and 400,000 people. Mostly human, a smattering of other races can be found here, but these nonhumans account for only 3% of the population. The city is perfectly circular, with the main arteries traversing from the central court in the center to the outer rim of the city, each street approximately one-half mile long and decreasing slightly in elevation. The lesser streets are circular, orbiting the central courtyard like a satellite.

Thief in the Night

The elves are approachable, stretching their arms out in friendship. The rangers claim to be on a mission to gain magical knowledge and ask the characters if they're citizens of Netheril. If the PCs say they're not, the elves ask if they wish to join in their search. The elves promise to share the information they gain if the PCs promise the same.

If the heroes agree to the terms, the elves claim that they're going to the Karsus Enclave to discover the secrets of Netherese spellcasting and invite the characters to go to Delia and enter the magic vaults of Lady Polaris. They give the PCs a map showing the details of the Polaris Vault and sketchy informa-

Central Courtyard

In the central courtyard surrounded by the street named Central Court, Lady Polaris has her castle, the Great Library, and the Polaris Vault. Along the perimeter of the courtyard, a two-man-tall wooden palisade is a deterrent to keep the common folk from entering the plush grounds of the palace.

Entrance

There's one entrance to the courtyard, and that's through the guardhouse on the northernmost part of the palisade. Thirty guards (all between 2nd and 7th level) and seven arcanists with *Smolyn's seer* and *detect lie* spells permanently cast upon their eyes

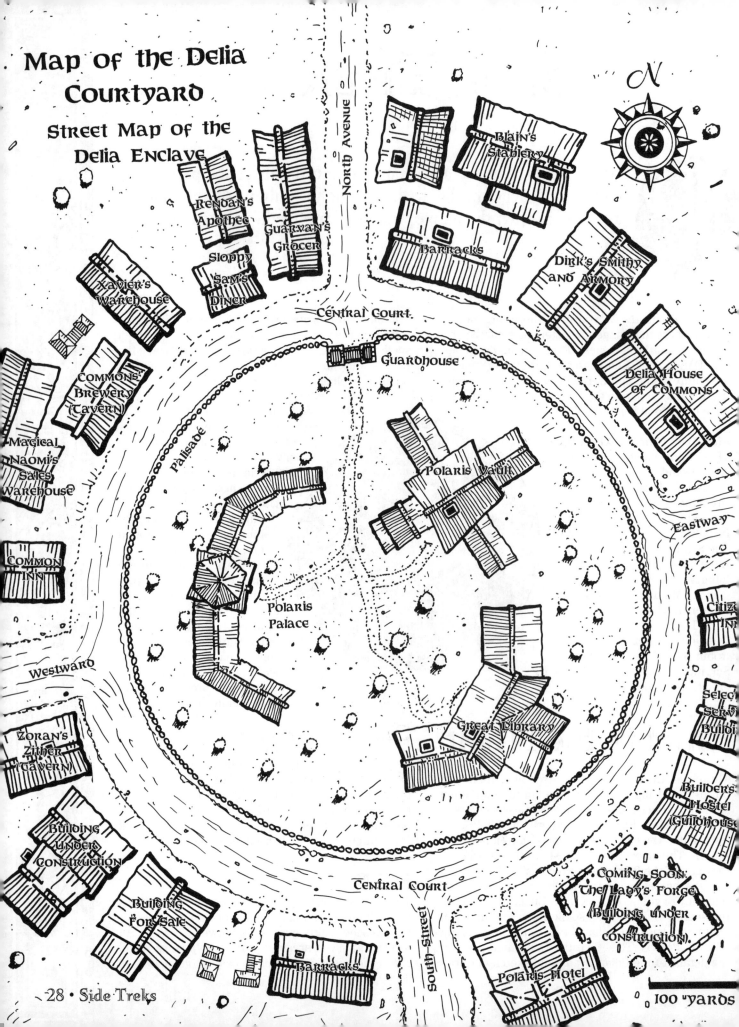

Map of the Delia Courtyard

Street Map of the Delia Enclave

Rendan's Apothec

Guarvan's Grocer

Sloppy Sam's Diner

Xavier's Warehouse

North Avenue

Blain's Stablery

Barracks

Dirk's Smithy and Armory

Central Court

Guardhouse

Commons Brewery (Tavern)

Delia House of Commons

Polaris Vault

Magical Naomi's Sales Warehouse

Palisade

Eastway

Common Inn

Polaris Palace

Citizen Inn

Westward

Zoran's Zither (Tavern)

Great Library

Select Service Building

Builders Hostel (Guildhouse)

Building Under Construction

Building For Sale

Central Court

South Street

Coming Soon: The Lady's Forge (Building under construction)

Barracks

Polaris Hotel

100 yards

question everyone who enters or attempts to enter the grounds. Those who do not "fit the bill" are ordered to leave, and arrested if they do not (should someone attempt to resist arrest, they're killed on the spot, with the body being sent to Rendan's Apothec for assimilation into grotesque and unusual potions and powders for use by the army stationed in the barracks).

The 12-foot-tall palisade, wooden in construct, is magically strengthened to the tensile strength of steel, meaning that it's immune to both mundane and magical fire and lightning. Magical cold, however, turns the wood brittle, allowing someone to smash it with a simple warhammer strike.

A magical current flows through each piece of wood in the palisade, originating from the eastern guardhouse and flowing around to the western guardhouse. If the current is broken, the guards send a unit of seven warriors and one arcanist around the inside of the fence to investigate the disturbance. If they find a break in the fence, the northern barracks (on the corner of Central Court and North Avenue) are alerted, and five units (35 warriors and five arcanists) are dispatched to find the intruders. Please note that a simple *dispel magic* disrupts the ward for 1d4 rounds.

If the fence is climbed and the villain carries magical items, three things can happen: quasimagical items are instantly relieved of their dweomer, true magical items must save vs. disintegration to maintain their magic (both done without the knowledge of the owner), and the climber must save vs. spell or be *paralyzed* until removed from the fence.

Magical means can be used to enter the fence, since this is one way that Lady Polaris enters and exits the compound whenever she wants to get away without the guards, the House of Commons, or the people knowing any better. Such ways include, but are not limited to: *Oberon's blinking*, *Oberon's teleportation*, *Shadow's walk*, and *Oberon's extradoor*.

Great Library

The Great Library is an absolute font of information. All documents (or copies thereof) made since the height of Netheril in 1964 NY are held here. All known spells, potion recipes, and religious and philosophical pamphlets and books created by Netherese are contained herein. As ordered by Lady Polaris, the library is categorized and indexed to death, making the location of desired information easy and quick.

During evening hours, the library is left unguarded by man. Instead, magic is used to maintain security. All windows are protected by an *Aksa's disintegration* spell activated by the decrease in light from the sun (easily overcome with a *Brightfinger's light* spell), the front door acts as an *Oberon's extradoor* that opens up into a high-security cell in the constabulary's jail house about seven blocks directly north of the Delia Courtyard (easily overcome by another *Oberon's extradoor*).

Once inside, all the PCs need to do is find the index books kept by the librarians a few dozen yards away from the front door to locate whatever information they require.

Please note that information about 11th-level spells and higher are not contained here. Instead, these high-level documents are kept in the Polaris Palace.

Polaris Palace

The only way into the Polaris Palace if the front door is not used, is through the use of a *gate* spell from another plane. Any attempt to magically teleport is met with a very unpleasant jaunt into the 43rd plane of the Abyss. If one climbs the walls to enter through the windows, they are met with a very unpleasant side effect: the walls and the roof are completely covered with an *Aksa's disintegration* effect—say good-bye to finger tips (or even whole bodies if one is thrown or pushed into the wall). One way past this is to a *Stoca's wings* or *Yturn's levitation* spell to a window or the roof. However, if the window is touched from the outside, the violator find himself securely glued to the window (much like the effect of *sovereign glue*); then it's only a matter of time before the magic that got the PC to the window wears off and he falls, striking the wall on his way down, disintegrating his body (up to the arm, at least, since his hands and fingers are still be attached to the window).

The front door is continually guarded by five warriors and one arcanist (again with *Smolyn's seer* and *detect lie* spells permanently adhered to their corneas). Five other groups of guards of equal numbers and profession walk about the palace, making sure no one attempts to gain entrance through thieving or magical skills.

Since no one has ever entered Polaris Palace without personal permission from Lady Polaris herself, it's unknown to this day what happens when a thief enter uninvited. One thing is known, however: seven known attempts from master thieves have been attempted, and the thieves were never heard from again. The DM is encouraged to be especially creative and cruel while maintaining one way to succeed—after all, that's one thing Lady Polaris personally made sure of. (By the way, all information regarding the 11th-level spells are always kept in her bedchamber. Good luck!)

Polaris Vault

The Polaris Vault has no windows and two doors on the eastern part of the central hub. Once inside, a visitor finds five different exhibits: the Warriorward, the Thief's Den, the Dweomercraft Auditorium, Divinetabla, and Polaris's Exhibit.

Divinetabla: This section mostly details the gods known in Netheril, including several worshiped by the nonhuman races Netheril has dealt with in the past. The remaining third of the exhibit details the magic and quasimagical items in use by the priesthoods throughout Netheril. This even includes the holy symbols and totems held dear to the religious icons of the gods' followers. Also included is a synopsis from Karsus of Netheril who claims the gods of Netheril are nothing more than frauds, which, by no surprise, has caused a great deal of stress among the religious sects. Many believe this single seven-page writ is the cause of all unrest in Netheril, since Karsus made it very clear that all archwizards believe the same thing.

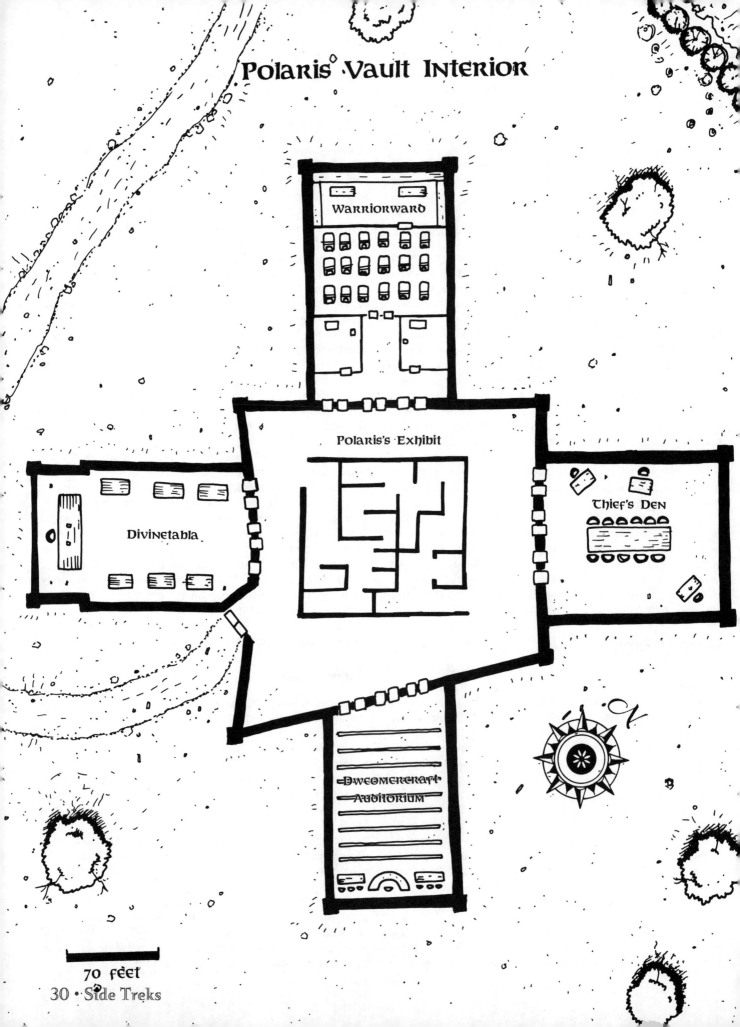

Polaris Vault Interior

Warriorward

Polaris's Exhibit

Divinetabla

Thief's Den

Dweomercraft Auditorium

70 feet

Dweomercraft Auditorium: This, the most crowded section of the vault, shows all the items, scrolls, and books usable by the spellcasters in Netheril. None of the *nether scrolls* are included in this exhibit.

Polaris's Exhibit: This special section in the center of the Polaris Vault displays the magical items created by Lady Polaris herself (though small in number), and all new exhibit pieces procured by the vault librarians. One interesting thing about this particular exhibit is that there are a number of books that detail the exact way to create spells in classic Netherese style—spells that contain no somatic components (**Note:** these five book are what the Cormanthyr elves desire to fulfill their quest.)

Thief's Den: This section of the Polaris Vault contains the least number of magical items and it's the only one that contains nonmagical items. Herein are all the items that a thief would use in his career. A section that takes up a third of the exhibit in the back contains the magical varieties known to Netheril. The remaining two-thirds shows the nonmagical varieties, from lockpicks to fantastic wall-climbing apparati. This is truly a study of the subversive when one steps in his hall.

Warriorward: This auditorium features all the magic and quasimagical items useful to the warrior, the soldier, and the nonspellcasting adventurer—at least those that are available in Netheril. Over 3,000 items are on display here, each with a description of the known functions and the creator.

As an extra level of security, Lady Polaris "hired" the help of some planar beings. About seven years ago during her planar travels, Lady Polaris discovered Mechanus and *gated* five decaton modrons from their home plane into the Polaris Vault, but she just couldn't figure out how to keep them contained in the building. For some unknown reason, the decatons would be in place for no less than five days before they'd disappear. She believed that Primus or one of the Secundi were responsible for the continual extraction.

She loved their lawful neutral attitudes and decided they'd be the perfect beings to use as security. The only thing she had to do was to find some other nonessential being to use for her security forces. On a return visit to Mechanus, she discovered the pentadron modron, and decided these beings could serve her needs. After *gating* them to the Prime Material Plane, she trapped them in the Polaris Vault, and there they remain, seven years later.

If someone enters the Polaris Vault during the off hours (sundown to dawn), the modrons attack.

Pentadron Modron (5): AC 3; MV 18; HD 5+5; hp 40; THAC0 15; #AT 5; Dmg 1d4+4(×5); SZ M; ML fearless (20); Int very (11); AL LN; XP 2,000 each.

SA: A save vs. paralysis is required to maintain motor control when attacked by the modron's paralytic gas stream (usable once every five rounds that extends 5' away from the modron with a 2-foot diameter); the gas stream can also be used to *levitate* the modron (as the 5th-level wizard);

SD: The modron saves vs. cold, fire, and acid with a +1 bonus; damage from such attacks have a –2 modifier per die; cannot be never surprised; they never roll for initiative—the DM determines when they attack; they have an effective 18/00 Strength; they have 180-foot *infravision*; immune to *beguiling, charm, domination,* emotion-altering effects, *fear, hold, hypnosis,* illusions, mind-affecting effects, *sleep*

A Thousand Fists Knocking

If the heroes investigate the noise, they see a group of 78 orcs—10 of whom are of huge stature and three who are dressed in wild, obnoxiously colorful clothing (shamans). The orcs apparently are going to sleep under the stars, but there are nearly 15 fires burning, each with a two-day supply of wood..

Spoken in Orcish, the characters hear these clips of speech: "…death to the Neth…," "…the only good human is medium rare…," "…if we swings south at Yeoman's Loft, we can easily raid Spiel in a fourday…," "…Me hears they's got pretty no-hairs [human females] there…," "…wish we'd've brought 'the dogs'…," "…me sword's hungry; me needs t' feed it…," "…ever tried their eyes served o'er iced gruel?…"

Orcs (65): AC 6; MV 9; HD 1; hp 6 each; THAC0 19; #AT 1; Dmg 1d8 (sword); SZ M (6' tall); ML elite (14); Int high (10); AL LE; XP 175.

Orogs (10): AC 3 (plate mail); MV 6; HD 3; hp 21; THAC0 17; #AT 1; Dmg 1d10+3 (sword + Strength bonus); SZ M (6'-7' tall); ML elite (14); Int high (11); AL LE; XP 65 each.

Orc Shamans (3): AC 6; MV 9; HD 5; hp 37, 33, 29; THAC0 15; #AT 1; Dmg 1d6 (club); SZ (6' tall); ML elite (14); Int exceptional (15); AL LE; XP 650 each.

Winds available (12/3rd): Transcendent, sporadic, wandering. Favorite spells: *command, protection from good, sanctuary; hold person; dispel magic.*

The orcs *refuse* to negotiate with humans, preferring to kill them on sight and use their possessions against the next batch of humans they run across. They believe all humans are Netheril citizens or simply descendants of the Neth, and as such, they're considered holy enemies, giving them a +4 attack bonus, much like the ranger special ability. This bonus is never applied to any opponent except humans.

If the PCs rush in to attack, the orcs create a horseshoe defense, hoping to surround the characters, with each PC suffering at least one orc strike per round. If the PCs attempt to attack them from the safety of the underbrush, the orcs rush in all directions, hiding in the bushes, trees, and just sneaking about.

Breaking and Entering

The characters are at the front door of Nopheus's home. The front door is the only solid-looking obstacle to the house. The five windows across the four walls all are covered with single-pane glass and dilapidated slats to help reduce winter draft.

If the characters break down the door, they're met with a *glyph of warding* that inflicts 20d4 points of electrical damage to all within 20 feet. If the windows are opened, one of four things can happen (depending upon which window is broken).

1. An alarm is set off, and the constabulary (1d8 5th-level warriors) appear within 1d4 rounds.

2. A *glyph of warding teleports* the violator 20–80 (2d4×10) feet into the air over the sharp rocks of the harbor. Damage is calculated using a single d6 for every 10 feet the character falls (8d6 maximum for this fall). In addition, the sharp rocks each inflict 1d8 points of damage, and the character strikes 1d4 of those when he finally comes to rest.

3. A *glyph of warding teleports* the violator directly into a cell of the Yeoman's Loft jail house on Helm Road north of Pine Forest Road.

4. A *glyph of warding* drains three levels from the violator. The victim is allowed a saving throw for each level removed.

Nopheus (NG hm F8; 72 hp) arrives (or wakes up), grabs *Twinrazor*, a *+3 bastard sword* (refer to the **Spells & Magic** section for information on *Twinrazor*), and seeks out those who would rob his home.

If the characters kill Nopheus, they've successfully destroyed the adventure, but in the process, they've gained *Twinrazor*, a fairly good Netherese weapon. They also gain the 2,000 gold he was planning on rewarding those who would return the body of his wife. Also, stashed in a safe behind a picture above the fireplace, the characters find three magical daggers, five other random quasimagical items, three scrolls bound into a book with five random 1st-level spells and the formulae for six additional cantras, and a gold foil etching of a beautiful woman (presumably his wife shortly before her death).

If the characters leave Nopheus's body to rot in the house, the constables find the remains three days later and investigate the death by means of a *speak with the dead* spell. With it, they discover and formulate well-rendered drawings of the murderers. If the characters are still in Yeoman's Loft, they discover their likenesses posted on trees, the doors of every tavern, and on the Neth Gatehouse. Within another threeday, their likenesses are scattered all across Netheril's enclaves and 30% of the ground-based cities. Another three days is all that's required to get their picture scattered throughout every Netheril city.

WANTED

For the murder of Nopheus of Yeoman's Loft, the bodies (dead or alive) of the villains pictured above are desired by the constabulary of Yeoman's Loft; for the price of 1,200 pieces of gold per face pictured herein.

So heinous was their crime of mutilation and death, these Criminals of Society must be considered highly dangerous and vile; though alive is desired, death is viable, for they can be resurrected to face the pain and long-suffering warranted by their actions in life.

• Days one to three: the PCs have a 10% chance per day of being spotted and recognized in Yeoman's Loft.

• Days four to six: There's a 20% chance per day of being spotted and recognized anywhere in Netheril.

• Days seven through nine: The PCs have a 40% chance per day to be spotted and recognized anywhere in Netheril.

As the days move forward, the characters can expect to meet more and more bounty hunters hungry for the reward, all intent upon killing the characters.

If the characters are still in Netheril after 12 days, an arcanist-turned-bounty hunter places a *Chevic's tracer* spell on the characters, allowing other hunters to *gate* right behind (or in front of) the characters at inopportune times. This treatment continues until they finally leave Netheril.

In Jail

If the characters end up in jail, chances are very good they deserve it. Below is a synopsis of the jail-term possibilities, depending upon the reasons they ended up in the jail in the first place.

• If they attempted to rob Yeoman's Bank, they were subjected to an *Oberon's teleportation* spell and transported to jail, arriving in a special cell dedicated to the thieves of that bank. When they appear there, they find seven others in the cell with them. The cell is cold and damp, with moisture clinging to the walls and a small pool of murky water sitting in the corner. It's safe for them to assume they're underground. The seven others (five males and two females) say they've been there for various terms: three of the men have been there for six months, the female and one male have been there for two years, and the remaining two have been there for five years. Each of the seven believe they have a full 10-year term to suffer through.

• If the heroes got involved with the assassination attempt on Karsus, they spend only three days in prison, for thereafter, they are rendered unconscious, all information about the underground sapped from their brains, and their essences (or what's left of them) relinquished to the planes of their deities.

When the cell door is inspected, a lock is discovered, but the lock isn't engaged. It doesn't need to be; two bars on the outside of the cell door have been welded into place in seven spots each, and an iron golem sits idly, across the hall, constantly vigilant, watching the prisoners with unblinking eyes.

Golem, Iron (1): AC 3; MV 6; HD 18; hp 80; THAC0 3; #AT 1; Dmg 4d10 (fist); SZ L (12' tall); ML fearless (20); Int non (0); AL N; XP 13,000.

SA: Breathes out a cloud of poison gas once every seven rounds (save vs. poison or die) that fills a 10-foot cube directly in front of it.

SD: Can be struck only by weapons of +3 or better enchantment. Immune to all spells except those based on electricity (which *slow* the golem for 3 rounds) and fire (which heal the golem on a one-to-one basis).

If someone attempts to break the welds (each requiring 100 points of bludgeoning damage), the golem reaches into the cell (its hand and arm fit perfectly though the cell door's grating) and tries to steal the weapon. If it's attacked as it attempts to steal the weapon, it withdraws from the attack and waits for swords and the like to be poked through the bars. Should this happen, the golem swipes at the blades; a successful hit snaps the blade at the bars, converting the weapon to a dagger with an extra-large hilt. If it's attacked a second time, the golem renders a *heat metal* spell, causing all metal, including the bars, to heat dramatically (see *heat metal* spell). When the *heat metal* spell is cast, it causes the welds and the bars to return to full strength.

When it's time for a prisoner to be released (10 years for attempted or successful robbery), the constabulary casts *Prug's hold human* spells on everyone in the cell, removes the welds, pulls out the newly-freed prisoner, reinstates the welds, and then simply allow the *Prug's hold human* spells to wear off. Meanwhile, the prisoners are fed twice per day and allowed water whenever they want through a small spigot in the wall.

The DM should come up with a way for the characters to escape, though no official way is documented here. Ideas range from *teleporting* to *gating*. Of course, if the PCs escape, so do the other convicts (and some of the heroes with more ethical outlooks on life might have a problem with releasing a thief into the streets).

The Search

To activate his 12th-level spell, Karsus needs the stone-filled gizzard of a gold dragon and part of the epidermis of the pituitary gland of the Tarrasque just to enchant one of the material components of the spell. Depending upon how evil the DM wants to be, he can choose to either send the PCs after the gold dragon or the Tarrasque (or even both).

The Gold Dragon

To reach the aerie of the gold dragon, the characters must expend a great deal of energy. Nonweapon proficiencies such as fire building, mountaineering, rope use, and survival (mountains) should be considered essential, whereas animal lore, cooking, direction sense, endurance, fishing, herbalism, hunting, jumping, set snare, and weather sense makes life on the hard mountains a great deal more comfortable. Several days hanging by ropes along cliff faces, sleeping in nooses and makeshift shelters with nothing but open air below makes the experience a memorable one.

When the DM has characters roll for mountaineering or rope use while climbing cliffs and the like, don't just assume that the character falls to his death immediately upon a failed roll. Instead, make his life just a bit more miserable. Items could fall out of backpacks, potions could get broken when the character smashes into the cliff face, and other calamities could befall the hero.

The journey to the lair of the gold dragon should take three or four days. The climb should be hard and tiring; player-characters should be truly grateful upon reaching the top of the mountain.

Entrance to the Lair

When the characters finally reach the lair of the gold dragon, there's a cloud giant named D'nascus asleep just inside the mouth of the cave. If the characters are wearing armor, try to don their armor, or are carrying armor, the sound of the clanking metal awakens the guardian. If they don't wake the giant and immediately attack him, they all have a free round of attack. Thereafter, however, combat runs in normal Initiative order.

If D'nascus awakens and the characters haven't attacked him yet, he demands that they state their purpose. If the characters admit that Karsus sent them, he grabs his morning star and prepares for battle. (Many adventurers have already approached Dracolnobalen in hopes of acquiring her gizzard, and D'nascus would rather die than let his companion fall to greedy humans). D'nascus is willing to listen to the adventurers if they are both honest about who sent them and admit that they aren't comfortable attacking Dracolnobalen.

If the PCs attack: The confrontation turns into a free-for-all, with Dracolnobalen arriving on the third round of combat to lend her breath weapon, spells, and claws to the combat. No quarter is given; it's a battle for survival.

> **D'nascus Cloudburst, male Cloud Giant:** AC 0; MV 15; HD 16+(1d6+1); hp 119; THAC0 5; #AT 1; Dmg 1d10 or 6d4 (huge morning star); SA +11 on all physical combat damage, hurl rocks for 2d12; SD Surprised only on a 1; SZ H (24' tall); ML Fanatical (17–18); Int Very (12); AL NG; XP 11,000.
>
> **Special Equipment:** *ring of fire resistance*
> Spells (9/2nd): 1st—*animal friendship, cure light wounds, invisibility to animals*; 2nd—*heat metal, slow poison.*

D'nascus Cloudburst has been a friend and companion to Dracolnobalen for several centuries. Back in their younger years, the two adventured throughout the continent, eventually graduating to the planes, having a particularly good time in the Elysium Fields and the Happy Hunting Grounds.

During one such visit to the hunting grounds, D'nascus fell victim to an aerial assault that left him for dead. Dracolnobalen scooped her fallen companion and flew him to the safety of a nearby mountain range and knitted his wounds. After three weeks of recovery, the dragon

gated back to Faerûn and continued to nurse the giant for four months.

D'nascus never forgot the deed, and vouched that day to remain with Dracolnobalen as companion, protector, and confidante for the remaining years of his life; thus far, he's thwarted 17 attacks from adventurers and gem-seekers in the last century and a half.

If the characters slay the dragon, it takes about one hour to cut through the dragon's skin, sift through the organs to find the gizzard. Please note the gizzard is the size of a medium bag (three feet long and two feet in diameter), weighing 150 pounds. If the characters don't have a magical item that can store the gizzard or a way to preserve it, they attract the attention of carnivores and scavengers throughout the trip back to Karsus.

> **Dracolnobalen, female, 397-year-old Gold Dragon:** AC –4; MV 12, Fl 40 (C), Jp 3, Sw 15; HD 20; hp 140; THAC0 –2; #AT 3+special; Dmg 1d10/1d10 (claws), 6d6 (bite); SA fire and chlorine gas breath (16d12+8 ea.); SD fear (90' radius); MR 50%; SZ 100' (body) + 93' (tail); ML fanatic (18); Int genius (18); AL LG; XP 20,000.
>
> **Notes:** Dracolnobalen gains a +8 to all combat modifiers (THAC0 listed above takes this modification into account); she casts spells as a 16th-level spellcaster; all of her spells have a Casting Time of 1 and she cannot perform any other function in the round when she casts. She can stall to create a dust cloud equal to her *fear* radius with a duration of one round—no combat or spellcasting is possible as all are blinded.

If the heroes negotiate: D'nascus agrees to lead the characters to Dracolnobalen so long as they place all of their armor and weapons into a large sack (that he carries). He warns the player-characters that draconic runes in the walls of the tunnel and in the lair itself spell certain death for spells cast by non-dragons (which isn't true; the runes are merely decoration).

When the heroes arrive at the lair of Dracolnobalen, they're greeted to the sight of an immense, glittering gold dragon that looks out at them with deep, wisdom-filled eyes. The ancient dragon allows the PCs to make the first offer, but she has no intention of laying down her own life for the "*human* kingdom of Netheril."

If the heroes can't come up with something of their own, Dracolnobalen offers a different path.

> "My mate, Argence, has gone to die. Unfortunately, we were not able to deal with the threat of the Tarrasque down in the valley of the Angardt barbarians. It will awaken soon, and when it does, many of the gentle barbarians will die. All will be forced to flee their lands."
>
> Dracolnobalen digs around in her treasure horde and produces an iron flask that contains a thick, syrupy liquid. "After battling the Tarrasque, pour this over its body. That will return it to its state of slumber."

Once this is done, Dracolnobalen promises to obtain the stone-filled gizzard of her mate. It's obvious that she finds this distasteful, but she'd rather suffer a little bit of heartache than to sit back and allow the barbarians to die.

Dracolnobalen won't pay the PCs in any other way; after all, they came to her for help. She isn't aware that

Karsus requires the pituitary gland of the Tarrasque to complete his latest spell. If informed of this, she's shocked that Karsus would awaken the creature just for a spell component. Still, that doesn't change the terms of her agreement.

The Tarrasque

On their way to the Angardt lands, the PCs run into groups of barbarians that can easily direct them to the "lair of the sleeping beast." Angardt legends claim that the creature's awakening spells doom to their people, and in recent months the barbarian shamans have been predicting the beast's awakening.

If the heroes state that they are returning from Dracolnobalen's lair with a gift from the dragon to make sure that the beast continues its sleep, the barbarians cheerfully lead the party to the burial mound containing the Tarrasque. The barbarians attack the heroes immediately if the PCs relate how they killed Dracolnobalen, whom they view somewhat as their protector.

The lair of the Tarrasque is an underground chamber surrounded by barbarian totems (set there to warn of the great evil within the mound). The site can be viewed from many miles away, as it sits on the low grasslands of the Neth Southwest. A variety of barbarian tents are situated around the lair of the Tarrasque.

These tents house shamans and warriors of the Angardt barbarians. Their duty is to keep an eye on the Tarrasque, fleeing to warn the rest of the tribe should it awaken. Part of their task entails keeping the torches in the beast's chamber burning, and this feat has grown into a test of bravery for both warrior, shaman, and arcanist alike.

There are 100 warriors, shamans, and arcanists at the mound, and they're not simply going to let anyone hop into the beast's lair and risk waking it up. PCs can convince the eldest shaman there to let them relight the torches. If they're arriving as part of an entourage with Dracolnobalen's gift, the shaman quickly agrees to let the heroes enter the lair. Of course, as the characters enter, most of the guardians withdraw a safe distance.

Once characters enter the mound, read the following:

> A giant chamber opens up into the earth below, a flickering of torch light casting haunting shadows along the walls. A slow, heavy breathing reverberates throughout the chamber.
>
> Laying upon a large dais in the center of the room is the huge form of a scaled creature. At least 50-feet long, its scales reflect the light of the torches and both of its white horns look strangely out of place in the gloom of the chamber—yet deadly.

The pituitary, located in the neck, can be accessed from the Tarrasque's current sleeping position, but if the characters begin to cut away at the creature with a nonmagical weapon, they discover that the only thing they do is wake the beast up. Magical weapons are required to affect the monster.

Once the Tarrasque has been awakened, it's a battle to the death. Should the characters decide that they're in over their heads, their only choice is to flee. If that's the case, the Tarrasque charges into the barbarian's tents, killing anyone it finds. It likewise pursues the heroes for five rounds, abandoning the chase whenever a more convenient target makes itself available.

Dracolnobalen is watching the player-character's progress. If the Tarrasque goes berserk, she *teleports* into the air nearby and aids the barbarians with a few well-placed breath-weapon attacks against the beast. The dragon only shows up as a last resort, however, most likely after a few of the player-characters have died.

Tarrasque (1): AC –3; MV 9; HD 70; hp 300; THAC0 –5; #AT 6; Dmg 1d12/1d12 (front claws), 2d12 (tail lash), 5d10 (bite), 1d10/1d10 (horns); SA sharpness bite, terror; SZ G (50' long); ML champion (15); Int animal (1); AL N; XP 107,000.

Notes: The tarrasque's bite acts as a *sword of sharpness*, severing a limb on a natural attack roll of 18 or greater; once every turn it can rush at MV 15, doubling horn damage and gaining a trample attack causing 4d10 points of damage; on sight, the tarrasque causes beings of less than 3 HD are paralyzed in fright and 3 HD or greater get a save vs. paralyzation to keep from fleeing in panic; its carapace reflects lightning bolts, all *cone* spells and effects, and *General Matick's missiles*—one in six reflect back at the caster causing normal damage; it's immune to all heat and fire; it *regenerates* 1 HP per round; only weapons enchanted +1 or higher can successfully strike the beast; it's immune to all psionics; the tarrasque must be brought below -30 HP for it to truly be dead and then a *wish*; spell must be used (the *wish* spell isn't created until a century after Netheril's fall, so it's impossible to effectively kill the tarrasque at this time).

To begin cutting the pituitary gland out without the use of a magical item requires the beast to be brought below –30 hit points. Until it's dead, magical weapons and magical attacks are the only way to harm the beast. The task of pituitary removal takes approximately one hour.

If the characters use *Aksa's disintegrate* to vaporize the remains of the Tarrasque once the pituitary gland is removed, they've created a problem for themselves. It *regenerates* from the largest existing piece of remaining flesh, which in this case is the pituitary gland, at the rate of one hit point per round, meaning that in 300 rounds (five hours) the Tarrasque is whole once again. The pituitary gland itself weighs 17 pounds and takes up about three large backpacks of space (it's pretty spongy material), which poses a small transportation problem for those who don't possess magical holding devices.

If the characters obtained Dracolnobalen's gift, they simply pour the flask over the Tarrasque (after it's been brought below –30 hit points, of course). Placing the body back on the dais might be a nice thing for the heroes to do as well, since if they leave it in the open it's bound to be disturbed earlier.

Once they bring both of the spell components back to Karsus, they can continue with their journey to rescue Amanda. They become Karsus's "very special friends" for a few days, and then the Archwizard commits himself to more research and experimenting.

Karsus Marketplace

The marketplace in the floating city of Karsus is full of vendors selling a multitude of goods. The streets are filled day and night; during the day, there are hundreds of people, while during the night, there are simply dozens. People of all standard PC races are found here as follows:

Below is a list of the types of vendors one finds here:

• Most prominent are peddler of quasimagical items (items that function only on floating cities). All these items can be bought for half the price listed in the ENCYCLOPEDIA MAGICA™ volumes. These vendors allow a bit of haggling, but never reduce their price more than 10%. Ninety percent of all vendors are magically protected versus charms and enchantments that force them to negotiate in a fashion positive to the buyer; 70% have audible alarms that activate a siren that screams whenever a spell or spell-like effect is activated against the vendor, which brings the city guards within 1d4–1 rounds.

• Real magical item vendors sell their items for 50% more than the price stated in the ENCYCLOPEDIA MAGICA tomes. They have audible alarms and protection just like other merchants.

• Exotic meats and vegetable sellers sell their meats for one-tenth the Experience Point total for defeating the creature for each pound. This price is negotiable by 25%.

• Spell component distributors sell their wares by spell level. Simply tell the vendor what spell is desired, and the components for that spell are sold in a small wrapped-and-tied packet at the price of 10 gp per spell level per spell. If specific components are desired, determine which spell the component is for and charge 2 gp per spell level for the component (ingredients bought in this way are sold loose). Spell components like gems are purchased elsewhere.

• Weapon vendors are somewhat popular, but what's for sale differs from enclave to enclave. Yeoman's Loft, for instance, does not allow the sale of polearms. Karsus Enclave allows the sale of all weapons, since it's so near the western frontier of Netheril.

• Clothes wholesalers are commonplace here as well. All the clothes are priced three-times the value stated in the *Player's Handbook*. The enchantments cast on the clothes reduce wear and tear, cause prismatic effects to dance across their surfaces, emanate magical colors, have magical properties to protect the wearer, or cause magical effects at the will of their wearer. (All such enchantments are quasimagical; treat the cost as 50 gp per spell level per spell).

In the marketplace, a number of opportunities arise for the characters:

☞ Karsus, always looking for dupes to perform his dirty work, sends a messenger for "the powerful-looking strangers" to see if they'll go on a quest for him. (Please note that he doesn't tell the characters who he is unless he thinks that's the only way for him to convince them to do the work. Refer to **The Search** on page 33.

☞ They see a note from the city of Vandal Station who're in need of the bravest souls in Netheril. If they decide to answer the call, refer to **Scrying the Orcs Through** on page 40.

Liberty on my Mind

There's a group of people on Karsus who've been looking for peace and freedom for nearly a decade, and their efforts have been fruitless. Only recently have their attempts turned desperate and violent. (The DM should refer to **Quelling the Serfs** on page 37, for these two adventures, though diametrically opposed, share much of the same information.)

If the characters have been sought-out by the constabulary, the Underground searches the heroes out and invites them to join their ranks. To prove their validity as freedom fighters, the characters are asked to perform a few jobs.

• A corrupt politician named Hrothard (NE hm F10) needs to be silenced, for he's forever spitting venomous rhetoric about the Underground and how they're nothing more than ruthless vagabonds without a goal. Adrian Freeman gives the characters a magical apple that they're to feed to the politician.

Once consumed, the politician's vocal chords are permanently silenced and his hands forget how to write. This effect is permanent and can't be removed short of deific intervention or the casting of a *wish* or *alter reality* spell (which haven't been invented yet).

• An important member of the Underground has been captured and his torture and mental probe is imminent. To maintain the security of the Underground, the PCs are asked to break the woman out of prison. Unfortunately, the jail house is manned by five members of the constabulary (NG hm F13, NG hm F12, LG hf F9, CG hf F8, CN hm F12) and one spellcaster (NG hf Variator10) who fight until their Morale (13) is broken. If the combat exceeds 12 rounds, the constabulary gains reinforcements of 2d4 more warriors of 2d4 levels and 1d2 spellcasters of 1d6+4 levels.

If captured, the characters' gear is taken and they're placed under heavy guard and sentenced to death (with the lethal task taking place in three nights). However, the Underground comes to their aid by digging a tunnel under the street to the cell. There's an 80% chance that the eight guards in the jail house notice the characters as they're leaving and they pursue them. A warrant and bounty for the PCs' arrest is issued.

If the PCs manage both tasks (while the Underground keeps a close eye on them through the use of divination spells and *crystal balls*), they're brought into the fold. They're given a book called the *Diary of Atrocities* to read that explains why the Underground exists. Through well documented and cross referenced sources, the book details the audacious crimes committed by the archwizards against the people of Netheril. Topics of murders, exiles to random planes and continents (and remote islands) of Toril, and segregation of impure humans to slums and rat-infested regions of the enclaves fill its pages. Every archwizard in Netheril has at least one such crime documented in the diary.

Once part of the team, they're brought into the Underground's greatest plan: the assassination of Karsus. At the point, the DM should refer to **Quelling the Serfs** on page 37.

Nether Here Nor There

The characters find a female woman adventurer dressed in a black leather outfit designed to thwart the effects of cold, heat, lightning, and other elemental, paraelemental, and quasielemental effects. (See **New Equipment** on page 56 for more information on the *Dying Woman's Leather Ensemble*.) The lady carries a small satchel on her left hip that appears undamaged and a severely nicked long sword that has a broken tip and a shattered hand guard.

The once-beautiful lady (LG, hf F13) bleeds from several holes and slashes in her body, most of which are along her face, neck, and midriff. She states that she was fighting a tanar'ri and managed to kill it before she fell, but there's no evidence of the fiend anywhere (since it returned to its home plane once it was destroyed on the Prime Material Plane). She declines all offers of healing, choosing instead to make sure she is "pure" for the afterlife (by not accepting healing magic).

She claims that she was on a mission from Lady Polaris to recover a cache of scrolls on the edge of the Far Horns Forest. Supposedly, the scrolls there were none other than the *nether scrolls*. As she passes from this existence, she asks the characters to finish her quest.

In her satchel, the characters find a one-foot square sheet of papyrus with a map, written in red ink. The map shows a small section of the Far Horns Forest with the city of Wreathe and the Purple Mountain Range as a guide and scale (no other scale is available on the map).

When the PCs get to the place on the map, they find a secret monastery dedicated to the worship of Mystryl. The magical monks aren't too happy to see the characters, but they've been expected for about 12 years. They serve the PCs a good meal and provide baths to break the road fatigue.

In the morning, the monks bring the characters a small, ornate chest (6″ W × 4″ H × 13″ L), and request they don't open the chest until they get to their destination. The monks state that by opening it, the scry-defeating magic will be dispelled, and anyone looking for the scrolls can able to find them.

During their trip, the DM should roll for random encounters once per day until they pass the Shinantra Mountains region when the random encounter rolls increase to twice per day. If the characters open the chest during their journey to Delia and Lady Polaris, they're met with daily (or even twice-daily) attempts on their lives by everything from tanar'ri to bandits in the employ of greedy arcanists who want the *nether scrolls*. If they don't open the case, the only thing they meet are the occasional wandering beast.

If the characters return the scroll case to Lady Polaris, she gives each one a magical device of their choice (up to the discretion of the DM). If the characters decide to hide the scrolls in order to have access to them in their own time period, it's up to the DM whether the scrolls survive discovery until then. He should keep in mind that over one millennia passes before the characters can hope to recover the scrolls, and a lot happens in the interim.

Quelling the Serfs

Karsus is always looking for adventurers, those who love law, and those who love Netheril and want to make sure it stays the way it was envisioned. Especially now, Karsus is looking for help in quelling the rebellion that seems to hover in the immediate future.

Karsus is convinced the rebellious nature of the new generation of Netherese is being instigated by a powerful lizardman from the Marsh of Simplicity. Many believe this lizardman (whose name has never been discovered) is as powerful a sorcerer as any archwizard, making him the most dangerous threat to Netheril in its long history. Karsus hopes to bring the characters to his side and have them infiltrate this subversive Underground, determine who the leaders are (at least in his enclave), and bring them to a swift and lethal justice.

Karsus offers each character, regardless of alignment and profession, 3,000 pieces of gold for this duty. As an added gratuity, Karsus promises to provide a salary bonus of 2,000 gold for each criminally treasonous individual they bring to justice. At this time, Karsus believes there are at least 40 persons that are riling the sentiments of the general populace, and the number could be well over ten-times that number. He makes his point that if the characters are completely successful, they could stand to make 800,000 gold pieces.

Karsus also warns the PCs that the group of instigators will undoubtedly lie to them in order to sway them to their side. He also tells the characters to watch out for the constabulary, because the guards are going to be looking for them, believing they are truly part of the rebellion. If caught, however, Karsus assures their escape which, in turn, will heighten the constables' awareness of the PCs. Karsus also warns to never kill a member of the constabulary, for their vengeance at that point becomes lethal and he won't be able to intervene in time.

While out in the streets, the characters see posters bearing their likenesses. Stated in the papers, the characters are wanted "alive" for crimes against the state. Many citizens who see them turn their faces and walk quickly away.

Yeoman's Loft Bank Interior

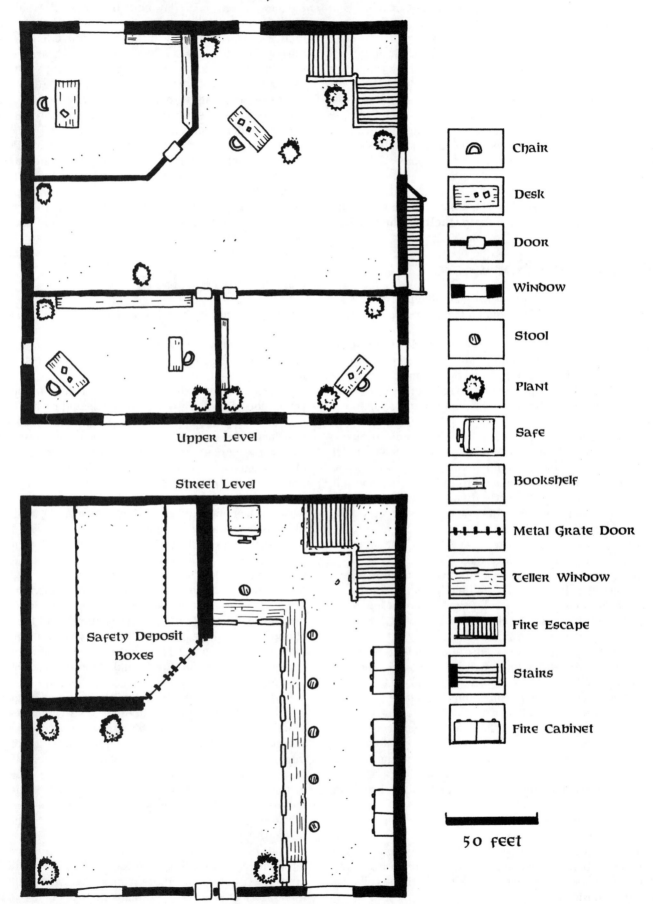

Upper Level

Street Level

Safety Deposit Boxes

Chair	
Desk	
Door	
Window	
Stool	
Plant	
Safe	
Bookshelf	
Metal Grate Door	
Teller Window	
Fire Escape	
Stairs	
Fire Cabinet	

50 feet

Each turn the characters remain on the street, they have a 20% to make contact with the constabulary who immediately give chase. To make matters easy, the DM should have each character roll a Constitution check. Rolling above a character's CON indicates capture. Each day the PCs are running from the law, the chance to meet the Underground increases 10%, beginning with a 20% chance the first day.

If a PC gets caught, Karsus uses *Oberon's teleportation* to excise them from prison during the night when none of the members of the militia are there to witness the escape. The destination point of the *teleportation* is the same location where the characters were arrested.

When the Underground finally approaches the PCs, they invite them to a little-used warehouse on the southern section of Karsus and search the PCs physically and magically for divination devices. If they find no such device or spell, they lessen their security and heave a sigh of relief. Adrian Freeman, the leader of the Underground, introduces himself to the heroes and begins speaking.

"Welcome, brethren, It's good to see others who seek liberty and justice from an oppressive dictator. It's good to see that some of us have read the banned and burned *Diary of Atrocities*."

If the characters are not familiar with this book and say so, the Underground members present seem shocked. Adrian Freeman then continues with his talk.

"It's hard to believe that you've joined the ranks of the Underground by your own fruition, but I guess it shouldn't be surprising. Netheril, after all, has created some of the most brilliant minds in the history of the world.

"As you apparently don't know, the *Diary of Atrocities* spells out the wrongs against the people of Netheril caused by the archwizards—murder, exiles, and segregation of impure humans to slums and rat-infested regions of the enclaves. Every archwizard in Netheril has at least one such crime documented in the diary."

Adrian Freeman gives them a copy of the book for them to peruse. If they decide to read the text, it takes three hours per individual. During this reading, they find details of crimes the archwizards executed against the people of Netheril. Some of the crimes include assassinating other archwizards, murdering people who questioned the authority of the archwizards, subjecting whole communities to magical diseases and ailments to "see what would happen," giving powerful quasimagical items with hidden effects to one side of a conflict in order to assure the extinction of unwanted "enemies," and using venerable and infirm persons as guinea pigs in horrid experiments.

If the characters maintain the illusion that they're on the side of the Underground, the rebels accept them into their inner chambers, located in the basement level of Adrian Freeman's home. Here, 45 people live, work, and plan their attack against Karsus.

The Underground plans to attack Karsus's castle in a threenight, hoping to catch him in his sleep so they can quietly assassinate him. Once the Archwizard is out of the way, the Underground plans on establishing their own leader (probably Adrian Freeman) to rule the people of the Karsus Enclave in a way the Underground believes is just and fair to all citizens.

Three days gives the characters plenty of time to warn Karsus and the constabulary of the plans. The exact plans are as such:

- The Underground *teleports* into Karsus's bedchamber.

- Four priests, one in each corner of the bedroom, cast *silence 15' radius* on themselves. Once cast, they all approach Karsus's bed and stand at each corner, effectively silencing the Archwizard.

- The five burliest warriors of the Underground each grab one of Karsus's appendages (each leg, two arms, and the head) and hold them down so he can't move or cast spells.

- An *amulet of life protection* is placed around Karsus's neck.

- Adrian Freeman, using a magical *dagger +5*, assassinates the Archwizard.

- Once death occurs, Karsus's essence is transferred from the body into the *amulet*. The amulet is then smashed, utterly and irrevocably destroying the psyche of Karsus.

Between the time that Karsus hired the characters and the planned assassination, Karsus' seers spot the clique of subversives and learn their plans. If the characters do not report their findings to Karsus before the day the plan goes into effect, he assumes (and possibly rightly so) that the Underground has poisoned their perceptions, and he writes the PCs off as new enemies. If the characters report this information to Karsus, they're given the job described for the constabulary below. If the characters join the Underground in the assassination attempt, they're considered part of the Underground.

A loyal servant to Karsus is dressed up in robes of state and is subjected to a *Quantoul's othermorph*, disguised to appear exactly like Karsus. This poor fellow is allowed to sleep in Karsus's bedchamber the night of the assassination, while the constabulary and a league of high-level spellcasters wait outside the bedroom. While lined outside the bedchamber, they whisper to each other until they feel the effects of the *silence*. Once this occurs, the spellcasters run to a room across the hallway and don *mantles* containing three *dispel magic* effects each that immediately disperse magical effects they contact and burst into the room.

The Underground has enough time to kill the impostor Karsus, trap his essence, and destroy the *amulet of life protection* before the constabulary and the spellcasters enter the room.

Underground (20): 1 F16, 3 F13, 2 A8, 8 F5, 6 F3
Constabulary (16): 1 F13, 2 F12, 3 F11, 4 F10, 6 F9
Spellcasters (8): 1 A15, 1 A13, 1 A10, 3 A9, 2 A8

As the constabulary and spellcasters burst into the room, the casters first fling themselves toward the Underground, dispelling all of the *silence* spells in effect. Normal combat ensues at this point.

If the characters are on the side of the Underground and they survive, they must find a way to escape. Refer to the Karsus Enclave map in the *Netheril: Empire of Magic* boxed set for information about the physical layout of the enclave. They are now wanted criminals with a 2,000 gp per level price on their heads! Refer to the end of **Breaking and Entering** for details on handling wanted characters.

Robin Banks

Nopheus's bank is located on the corner of Shadowtop Road and Aeroroad. The building looks rather small; a two-story stone-framed business with thick—very thick—windows on the store front and none on any other face. The second story contains two windows on each wall and a fire escape on the southeastern wall (the fire escape can be reached if a character can jump up or be boosted nine feet in the air).

The front door is locked with a lock which imposes a –20% penalty to a thief's *open locks* skill check. All the windows are thick glass that require 20 hit points of bludgeoning or 40 points of slashing damage to break. If the PCs break the glass on the first floor, they set off an alarm in the office of the nearest constabulary (eight 4th-level fighters), who respond to the intrusion in 2d4+8 rounds. If the characters merely slip tools into the door lock or break the windows on the second floor, they're able to gain entrance.

If the characters break into the second floor, they're relatively safe. Nothing can get them into trouble here. They can root through the desks, shuffle the books about, and walk down the stairs in complete safety. If they have lamps and pass by any of the windows, however, there's a 5% chance per incident that a guard notices the light in the window and sets off a general alarm.

If the characters are downstairs, things become a bit more dangerous. Behind the teller windows they find three, two-tiered cabinets. They can safely rifle through these, finding papers about the personal finances of those who use the bank to store their personal property.

The main safe has a tumbler lock mechanism that is magically enhanced, which creates an additional –20% penalty to any lock picking attempt. If the thief fails, he's immediately *teleported* to the jail. Anyone who reaches into the safe to pull out a set of 266 keys, 1,500 gold, 1,000 platinum, 4,575 copper, or 2,800 silver pieces without first whispering "I work for Yeoman's Bank," is likewise *teleported* to jail.

In the main lobby, the characters see a metal grating door that protects the main vault. Through the grating, they can see hundreds of safety deposit boxes. There's another magically enhanced lock on the door. Touching the lock or the door during nighttime hours without saying "I work for Yeoman's Bank" causes the thief to *teleport* to jail.

If the characters manage to safely bypass the grated door, they face 266 safety deposit boxes. Each box has two locks—one key for each is kept in the safe behind the teller windows, and the other is kept in the hands of the safety box renter. Touching any of these boxes causes the character to *teleport* to jail. If any of the Bigby's hand spells or nonliving items (dagger tips) are used to touch the boxes, however, the PC is not *teleported*; though all it takes is the slightest touch during nighttime hours to *teleport* the thief.

If the characters manage to break into the safety deposit boxes, roll on the table below to determine the contents:

% Roll	Contents
01-30	Paper (deeds, contracts, wills)
31-50	Paper (business documents)
51-60	2d20 gold pieces
61-65	1d4 platinum bars (5,000 gp each)
66-70	3d100 sp, 2d100 cp, 1d100 gp
71-75	1d4 gold bars (each worth 1,000 gp)
76-80	1d4 random, yet small, magical items
81-90	2d100 Gold, 4d20 platinum pieces
91-00	Empty

Scrying the Orcs Through

An outpost in the Neth Northwest, Vandal Station, has noted orc movements north of the Narrow Sea. It appears that the orcs are planning to head south when the Narrow Sea freezes over in midwinter. Over 4,000 strong, these orcs can inflict a great deal of damage as they pillage food from the laborious Netherese farmers and ranchers and supplies from the merchants and general populous.

The outpost sends word out to all of Netheril, looking for brave souls to avert this impending doom.

To the Brave and Adventurous

The sentinels of Vandal Station plead for your assistance! Never in the last 20 years has a horde so large and so menacing been at our northern border! Should they succeed in their quest, thousands of Neth shall starve in the winter's fury and hundreds more of Netheril's hardest working farmers and ranchers shall lie dead in the snow, assuring light harvests and even more deaths in the upcoming winters.

We plead your assistance! If you have spare time and a strong sword arm, we beg of you to head north or enter a Neth Gatehouse to Vandal Station and aid us in our time of need!

When the PCs arrive at Vandal Station, they find a small, quiet community dedicated to guarding Netheril's interior from orcs and other invaders. The merchants sell the best *crystal balls* and divination equipment (at only 75% the normal prices found in the ENCYCLOPEDIA MAGICA tomes or the DUNGEON MASTER® *Guide*) that can be found in Netheril, and all of these accouterments are used by the diviners.

When the adventurers tell someone why they're in town (to do away with the orc threat), they're immediately sent to the center of town to a building called the Scry Conclavence. In this large, five-story building most of the seers (herein called Scrymasters) perform their activities in seclusion from the rest of the town.

When the characters are led into the building, the seers are fascinated by their heroism and ruggedness and demand (in awe) to hear their stories. Once the character tell them of their feats, the scrymasters settle down to business.

"The orcs in the Rengarth Tundra are planning a huge offensive gauged to begin once the thin sea between Northreach Sound and Annagoth Bay freezes over, allowing their dogsleds and their siege equipment to be safely transported to our side of the sea. Scrymaster Barren states that the orcs are planning to besiege the city of Northreach first, killing all the city's inhabitants in order to take their winter supplies. Northreach's destruction will feed the orc horde until they can reach our city—they've always hated us because we've kept an eye on their movements.

"Once Vandal Station is taken, they'll head south through the Rengarth Ancestral Lands where they have an open path to our grain fields and silos. When they take what they want and burn the rest, Netheril will be in terrible shape.

"We need a group of adventurers to enter the ranks of the orcs and assassinate their leaders. This will create dissension and panic in the ranks which will—hopefully—cause them to rethink their diabolic plans. Will you help us?"

If the characters agree to aid the scrymasters in this quest, they set the characters up with *crystal balls* which will aid them in discovering who and where the orc leaders are. They're also given *warmthstones* (detailed in the **Spells & Magic** chapter), warm gloves and clothing, and enough supplies (in a *bag of holding*) to feed all the characters for three weeks.

The PCs are led to a high-keeled boat lined in sealskin and they set afloat in the Narrow Sea, heading north-northeast toward the Rengarth Tundra about 30 miles north of Annagoth Bay. Even in late autumn, the weather is cold.

The trip across the water takes a little more than two days, and they arrive near dusk. The ground is slushy and partially solid with iced mud. Frozen reeds stick up from this liquid base, breaking off whenever the characters brush against them (creating a path behind).

Islands of solid ground can be found, and the PC's guide, Denias Fangkiller (CG hm F12/A14), leads them to one such isle and sets up camp by activating the *warmthstone* and pulling out his bedroll and climbing into it. It's plain to see that he's planning on letting the characters set up watch—unless he's asked to participate.

In the morning, Denias wakes up, deactivates the *warmthstone* and eats a small meal from the *bag of holding*. When everyone is ready to begin, Denias heads north-northeast at a fast pace (nearly running). At the end of the day, the characters and their guide again bed down for the night, but this time, Denias offers to keep first watch.

During the next day, the PCs travel for only six hours before Denias stops and declares that the orcs are holed up about one hour ahead. They can continue for another half hour before Denias stops and gives the characters the opportunity to do one of two things: they can either continue forward as they are, or they can use *Quantoul's othermorph* on themselves to change into orcs in order to fit it better (though explaining why they're not of the tribe may be a bit difficult). If the PCs have a better idea, Denias is willing to trust their judgment.

Going in as orcs: The PC-orcs approach the camp and are immediately intercepted by the orcs. They're taken to the leader once they've been stripped of their packs and weapons (though a suitably haughty PC can probably bluff his way out of surrendering his weapons, demanding to see the chief instead). As they make their way to the leader's tent, they see thousands of orcs scattered around. The leader and his council of eight elite warriors ask why they're there.

If the characters stand dumbfounded (since many of them probably don't understand the orcish tongue), Denias Fangkiller interjects and states. "Great leader, we're here because we've heard that you're going south to bring down the infestation of humans under the Great Sea, and we want to lend our lives in this pursuit."

If the characters say something along these lines as well, the orc leader looks at them for about two minutes before he says, "Prove your prowess..." At that instant, they're led outside, given their weapons, and then beset by a number of orcs equal to their numbers. If they all succeed and none are killed, the orc leader allows them to join once they take this oath of fealty:

"I, [name], hereby promise by life, my soul, and my arms to the service of the Great Deathdealer, Grask'ar, and vow to follow his every word and command as though it came from the great orc god, Gruumsh. To this I avow!"

If they say this with conviction, they're accepted into the ranks. Their remaining possessions are returned, and the heroes are given a place near the center of the orc encampment.

If the characters refuse to speak the vow (or just don't put much fervor behind their words), one or more of the PCs fall in the battle, or they admit that they're going to kill the orc leaders, they're met with wave after wave of orcs who're intent upon slaughtering each and every one of them. There are 4,000 orcs in this encampment, and each fights to the death in this instance. The PCs will have a huge fight ahead of them if they choose this path (and the orcs will try to overbear the heroes first, resorting to melee combat only if they can't succeed in overpowering them).

Going in as themselves: If they're spotted by sentries, the orcs scream out an alarm that would wake the dead, alerting all of their compatriots to the whereabouts of the human invasion. Half of the orcs in the camp move toward the heroes while the other half surround the tent of their leader, filling the tent with about 70 orcs to protect Grask'ar in case teleportation magic is used against them.

If the character are careful and sneak in like good little thieves, they can elbow up a small tor to look down upon the camp and use their divination items given them to find out exactly where the leaders are—the leaders are about seven tents from the exact center, in the third largest tent in the camp. From this vantage point, the characters can either use *Oberon's teleportation* spells to enter the leader's tent, or await darkness to enter and perform their task.

When they enter the tent, they find one huge orc (the leader), eight large orcs (shamans) and 10 normal orcs.

Grask'ar, Orc Chief: AC 4 (10); MV 9 (12); HD 3; hp 21; THAC0 17; #AT 2; Dmg 1d10/1d10 (sword); SA +2 Strength bonus on all attacks; SD 45% hide in shadows and natural surroundings, +1 save bonus to charm-related effects; SZ M (6' tall); ML champion (16); Int exceptional (16); AL LE; XP 65.

Orc Shamans (8): AC 6; MV 9; HD 5; hp 27 each; THAC0 15; #AT 1; Dmg 1d6+1 (mace); SA +2 attack bonus when they have surprise and/or their opponents are on lower ground, spell use; SD 45% hide in shadows and natural surroundings, +1 save bonus to charm-related effects; SZ M (6' tall); ML elite (13–14); Int exceptional (15); AL LE; XP 650.
Spells (12 winds/3rd): Treat the orcs as priests of Targus.

Orcs (10): AC 6; MV 9; HD 2; hp 14; THAC0 19; #AT 1; Dmg 1d8 (sword); SA +2 attack bonus when they have surprise and/or their opponents are on lower ground; SD 45% hide in shadows and natural surroundings, +1 save bonus to charm-related effects; SZ M (6' tall); ML elite (13); Int high (10); AL LE; XP 175 each.

• If the PCs manage to kill all of the leaders without setting off an alarm, the orcs are sufficiently demoralized and the scheduled attack is averted—until next year.

• If the PCs attempt to murder the leaders but fail, the orcs move up their attack to pre-winter, launching their assault from boats instead. During this time, all the orcs have a 16 Morale.

• If the PCs slay the leaders but are caught, they're beset by every orc in the community. They send out the call to all the other orcs in the Rengarth Tundra, telling them of the atrocity. This doubles their number, and they march on Netheril, beginning their assault in nine days.

THE LICHLORD'S CASTLE

Destiny in and of itself is a strange and powerful force. More adventurers have died trying to escape what must be than have ever died at the hands of some terrible monster. The trick, of course, is choosing one's own fate while fulfilling one's destiny.

End of the Journey

By the time characters arrive at this point, they should have already been given the opportunity to obtain Karsus' spell components for his *avatar* spell. As noted previously, Karsus sent a number of adventurers out to retrieve spell components; if the party refused to work for Karsus then one of the other adventuring groups succeeded in the heroes' stead.

Dead Denizens

As the characters near their destination, they run into three spellcasting followers of the Lichlord. The arcanists, intent on stopping—or at least delaying—the characters, have covered themselves in *dust of disappearance*. Even with this advantage, the arcanists still hide in the trees and for the first few rounds, project spells and magical item effects toward the PCs from the safety of height to weaken them and make their chance for success that much greater.

Dr. Killdrum, hm, Inventor15: AC 0 (*bracers of defense AC 2, cloak of protection +2*); MV 12; hp 45; THAC0 16; #AT 1; Dmg 1d4+3 (*dagger +3*); SZ M (6' tall); ML 15; AL NE; XP 10,000.
STR 14, DEX 13, CON 18, INT 19, WIS 17, CHA 11.
  Special Equipment: *Dr. Killdrum's wand of fire* (see the **Spells & Magic** chapter) is imbedded in his right arm, a *wand of lightning* (16 charges) hides under his tunic, and a *staff of the magi* (20 charges) serves as a walking stick.
  Spells (94/7th): 1st—*General Matick's missile, Primidon's burners, Carbury's servant, General Matick's armor, General Matick's shield;* 2nd—*Tolodine's stinking cloud, Primidon's sphere, Polybeus's illumination, Fahren's darkness, Shan's web;* 3rd—*dispel magic,*

Primidon's arrow, Gwynn's vampirism, Noanar's fireball, Volhm's bolt; 4th—*Lucke's contagion, Noanar's shield, Noanar's wall, Veridon's storm, Stoca's feign;* 5th—*Mavin's iron wall, Mavin's stone wall, Shadow's door, Tolodine's cloudkill, Veridon's cone;* 6th—*Dethed's spell, Volhm's chaining;* 7th—*Dethed's death finger, Noanar's delayed fireball, Valdick's force cage.*

Dr. Killdrum is a man who looks out for two things: his personal comfort and revenge. His loyalties at this point are with the Lichlord because he hopes to sate his greed for knowledge of magic that's currently out of his reach.

Dr. Killdrum once was an apprentice to the great Lady Polaris, but his fight for personal power and greatness eventually forced Polaris to eject the fledgling archwizard from her home. Revenge now sits in the forefront of his vicious mind.

Dr. Killdrum joined with the Lichlord because he was led to believe the lich was planning to attack Polaris's enclave (Delia), and he planned to set himself in her throne. Unfortunately, his plans are now on hold, because the Lichlord is going after the Archwizard: Karsus.

Krystaufer, hm, Mentalist14: AC 5 (*ring of protection +2*); MV 12; hp 42; THAC0 16; #AT 1; Dmg 1d6+4 (*staff +4*); SZ M (5' tall); ML 14; AL CE; XP 9,000.
STR 12, DEX 17, CON 16, INT 17, WIS 17, CHA 12.
  Spells (85/7th): 1st—*Keonid's charm human, Quantoul's changer, Trebbe's scry magic, Trebbe's scry identify;* 2nd—*Cragh's deafness, Enollaf's aimlessness, Hamring's enfeeblement, Keonid's forgetfulness, Smolyn's blindness;* 3rd—*dispel magic, Keonid's suggestion, M'dhal's missile shield, M'dhal's dispel evil II, Zahn's hearing, Zahn's seeing;* 4th—*Berthot's blunder, Keonid's fear, Oberon's extra door, Trebbe's minor invulnerability;* 5th—*Berthot's disorder, Hamring's feeblemind, Prug's dominate, Undine's avoidance;* 6th—*Smolyn's eyebite, Trebbe's invulnerability;* 7th—*Trebbe's turning.*

The Undead Castle

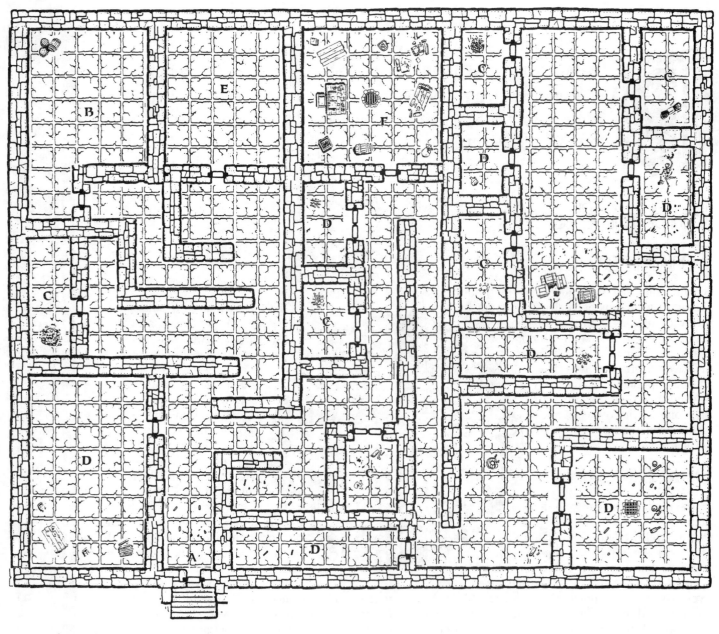

A. Entrance

B. Throne Room

C. Cell, Occupied

D. Cell, Empty

E. *Mythallar*

F. Laboratory

5 feet

Most people never know how to act or react around this man. His motivations and responses seem to change more than his eyes blink. One moment he's calm and collected; the next, he's wildly out of control.

Edie Savage, hf, Variator13: AC 4 (*bracers of defense AC 4*); MV 12; hp 39; THAC0 16; #AT 1; Dmg 1d4+2 (*dagger +2*); SZ M (5 ½' tall); ML 13; AL NE; XP 8,000.
Str 15, Dex 13, Con 14, Int 17, Wis 18, Cha 16.
  Spells (78/6th): 1st—*Nalevac's spray, Primidon's burners, read magic, Veridon's chiller, Yturn's feather fall, Volhm's grasp;* 2nd—*Aksa's shatter, Fahren's darkness, Quantoul's strength, Undine's extra portal pocket, Vilate's restriction;* 3rd—*dispel magic, Nalevac's deep sight, Quantoul's fastmorph, Tolodine's gust of wind, Quantoul's slowmorph;* 4th—*Quantoul's manymorph, Quantoul's othermorph, Quantoul's selfmorph, Lucke's contagion;* 5th—*Fjord's animation, Oberon's teleportation, Proctiv's rock-mud transmution, Undine's avoidance;* 6th—*Mavin's stone-flesh transmution, Aksa's disintegrate.*

Edie Savage was the apprentice and lover of the arch-wizard Ioulaum, but a spat over the dispensation of over-paid taxes rendered their relationship useless. Once they split up, Edie still haunted Ioulaum, pulling petty pranks in order to get the people of his enclave to distrust or hate the Father of Netheril. Still angry with the split and the fact she received nothing in the breakup, she takes her anger out on anyone who poses as a victim.

Setting Up The Ambush: The three wizards are in the branches of the trees along the characters' path, invisible even to one another. As the characters approach, they each have a detailed attack sequence. The DM should follow this plan as close as possible.

Round 1:
• Dr. Killdrum casts *Noanar's fireball*. He moves onto a different branch in case someone noticed him, but he stays in the same tree.
• Krystaufer casts *Trebbe's invulnerability* on himself. He jumps down—quietly—from his tree and approaches the PCs from their left flank.
• Edie Savage casts *Tolodine's gust of wind* shortly before the effect of Dr. Killdrum's *fireball* has ended. This helps fan the flames as well as its normal effect, allowing the flames to engulf more of the forest. She climbs down and approaches the characters from their right flank.

Round 2:
• Dr. Killdrum casts *Polybeus's illumination*, on a spell-caster (someone not wearing armor).
• Krystaufer casts *Smolyn's blindness*.
• Edie Savage casts *Hamring's enfeeblement*.

Round 3:
• Dr. Killdrum casts *Mavin's stonewall*.
• Krystaufer casts *Smolyn's eyebite*.
• Edie Savage casts *Mavin's stone-flesh transmution* in its reversed form.

Round 4:
• Dr. Killdrum casts *Volhm's bolt*.

• Krystaufer casts *Keonid's charm human*.
• Edie Savage casts *Quantoul's fastmorph*.

Round 5:
• Dr. Killdrum casts *Noanar's fireball*.
• Krystaufer casts *Keonid's forgetfulness* on a PC.
• Edie Savage casts *Quantoul's slowmorph*.

Round 6:
• Dr. Killdrum casts *Noanar's delayed fireball*.
• Krystaufer casts *Cragh's Deafness*.
• Edie Savage casts *Aksa's Shatter*.

Round 7:
• Dr. Killdrum casts *Veridon's cone*.
• Krystaufer casts *Prug's dominate* on a PC to force him into performing unusual tasks, like attacking someone in the PC's party.
• Edie Savage casts *Aksa's disintegrate* on a player-character weapon.

Round 8:
• Dr. Killdrum casts *Noanar's fireball*, centering the effect on as many PCs as possible.
• Krystaufer casts *Berthot's blunder*.
• Edie Savage casts *Lucke's contagion*.

Round 9:
• Dr. Killdrum casts *Tolodine's cloudkill*.
• Krystaufer casts *Enollaf's aimlessness*.
• Edie Savage casts *Quantoul's othermorph* hoping to transform the PCs into snails.

Round 10:
• Dr. Killdrum casts *Dethed's spell*.
• Krystaufer casts *Keonid's fear*.
• Edie Savage casts *Quantoul's manymorph*, hoping to turn the PCs into harmless rabbits.

Round 11+
If the characters haven't died or turned tail and run by this time, the DM has the option of continuing the combat, or having the NPCs leave the combat area to establish another ambush later. So long as the Lichlord's servants remain alive, they continue to attack the heroes, augmenting their attack plan each time based on their experiences with the player-characters.

Castle Approach

As the characters begin ascending a large hill in the forest, they come across a battalion of 12 undead, all lead by a ferocious (once-female) human. She has long and tangled brunette hair, whose tresses are held together by the web of some forest spider whose home is deep within her disheveled mane. Her clothing, resembling harlot livery, is a tattered and dirty gown of white. She displays a beautiful necklace over her crumbling frock that possesses a large blood red ruby surrounded by the silvery web of a black widow.

For the astute character, the necklace is a sign that the undead zombie woman they face is Amanda, Nopheus's wife. When she was resurrected from the ground into the ranks of the Lichlord's troupe, the preservation magic Nopheus purchased was eradicated, rendering his former wife to the wills of the elements.

When Amanda and her troop of zombies notice the characters, they attempt to surround the heroes and attack.

Amanda (Zombie): AC 6; MV 9; HD 9; hp 63; THAC0 12; #AT 2 or 1; Dmg 2d4/2d4 (fists) or 1d10/2d6 (halberd); SA 30' *control* of nonthinking undead; SZ 6'; Int 10; AL NE; XP 650.

Personality: Amanda remembers most of her former life in the realms of the living, but she knows she's dead and she "knows" there no way back and she's accepted her fate—in fact, she likes this new state of affairs. After all, she's not the bored housewife of a rich merchant and just the mother to unsavory children any longer. She doesn't have to go to business parties and dinners as a object of beauty to help make a sale, and her life is no longer dedicated to her former husband and their three children. In this new lease on life, she's now a leader of 12 zombies who do her every bidding without regard to limb and unlife. She'd rather have her unlife ended as opposed to going back to that kind of self-enacted oppression.

Generic Netherese Zombie (12): AC 6; MV 9; HD 6; hp 42; THAC0 15; #AT 2; Dmg 2d4/2d4; SA can *control* any nonthinking undead within 30 feet; SZ 6' tall; ML n/a; Int 9; AL NE; XP 650.

Capturing Amanda

The characters have a feisty undead on their hands. She attempts to break her restraints at all times, planning to crush the skulls of every character if she gets half a chance. When they near the Lichlord's castle, she commands all undead within her 30' radius of control, by silent will, to attack the PCs.

If the PCs cast a *resurrection* spell on her, she is returned to the realm of the living. This puts a temporary hold on her connection to the Negative Material Plane. This partial link remains throughout her life unless a *remove curse* spell is cast on her. This link causes Amanda to transform into a Neth zombie upon her death (regardless of the cause).

If the characters kill Amanda and then cast a *resurrection* spell on her corpse, she returns in all her beauty, her link with the Negative Material Plane forever severed. She thanks the player-characters profusely for their thoughtfulness, but she really has no idea what lies beyond her station (this is as far as she has traveled).

The Lichlord's Castle

As characters finally crest the hill where they fought the zombies, read the following:

The crest of the hill opens onto a valley that is bathed in gloom and fog. Deep within its center rests a huge castle made of some multicolored substance that emits a somewhat obscured glow in the embrace of the misty vapors. A walled pathway curves through the valley, leading to the main gates of the castle.

Travel into the valley is free of encounters; all natural wildlife and lesser monsters have been driven away by the Lichlord's presence. As characters approach the castle, read the following:

A horrifying revelation strikes your tired minds: the castle is not constructed of standard materials. Instead, it's assembled with the bodies of the living dead. Without blinking, the decaying bodies stand about unmoving; pillars wrapped in the flowing mists. Their collapsed, mustard-drooped eyes keep a constant vigilance on the landscape.

The cadavers stand in two rows, shoulder to shoulder and each carrying bladed pikes, outlining a crooked pathway that leads to a roughly circular wall three bodies deep and two high. The castle, also constructed of undead, towers 13-corpses tall within the wall. An unearthly, eerie blue light permeates the gaping chests and leg bones. As you look at the disgusting sight, eyes in the pathway, the wall, and the castle all turn to watch your every move.

The undead that create the castle cannot be turned or destroyed by any means save physical combat; clerical turning has no effect on them. If characters approach the castle, one of two things can happen, depending upon their actions earlier in the module.

The PCs helped Derf (page 24): The heroes have aided themselves in their quest. When Derf returned to the ranks of the Lichlord, he reported that the PCs were his friends and should not be attacked. As the PCs approach, the zombies nearest them smile, bow their heads, and say, "Derf sends you his best." They're able to walk through the front door unmolested. While they tour the undead castle, they're watched, but not told where and where not to go.

The PCs did not help Derf: As they approach the undead-lined pathway, the lead zombies move to stop the heroes. The Neth zombies ask in a ghastly chorus, "What do you seek?"

If the PCs say that they want to speak to the Lichlord, the undead pause for a moment (as their message is transferred to the Lichlord) and await a response. After a few moments, the undead allow the party to go through. As the characters walk through the castle, the zombies in the walls, floor, and ceiling instruct them where to go in order to find the Lichlord.

Within the Castle

The Lichlord uses his castle as an area from which he can operate without fear of interference from any archwizard who might come to investigate. He's already assimilated many of the troops sent against him, and any creatures who venture too close can easily be transformed into Neth zombies, which just makes him that much more powerful.

Attacking the zombie walls: If the characters decide to attack the zombies used in the castle's construction, they find that the undead are able to reconstruct the castle—changing the formation of the rooms and hallways. They can even open up the floor (either right from under the PCs

or to stop their flight). They can change the height of the ceiling in order to give the undead six forms of attack: above, below, to both sides, the front, and from the back.

A. Entrance

The mass of zombies part to reveal a pathway roughly 10-feet wide that stretches off into the heart of the castle. The strange blue light that hovers within each of the zombies provides the only means of illumination.

The first large cell to the left of the entrance hall is barely visible as the player-characters walk past. Treat the entrance into the cell as a concealed door.

B. Throne Room

The mass of twisted zombie bodies parts to reveal a large chamber that is mostly empty of furnishings. A huge, skeletal throne wrapped partially in rags is its only object of interest.

Seated upon the throne is a skeletal creature dressed in a tattered gray robe. Its eyes blaze with an orange-red light and rings adorn its fingers. Its voice, ancient and commanding, echoes forth in the eerie chamber.

"What can I do for my esteemed and brave visitors? I must admit to a lack of courtly manners, as I see and tend to few guests. It seems that few are able to see past the castle gates to visit me." The creature's cold and lifeless gaze slowly settles upon each of you.

The Lichlord has allowed the player-characters this far because he wants to know where their loyalties lie—are they for him or against him; perhaps they're ambivalent about the entire matter. So long as he feels they're up front with him about their intentions, the Lichlord answers virtually any question put to him.

• **Why the undead army:** "I am able to control an army of undead to do my every bidding. The living, especially humans and elves, tend to view their personal agendas and greed with more importance than the needs of the many. This means they cannot be trusted. Therefore, I was forced to create my own army. These bodies were not being used, and I hate to see anything go to waste."

• **Are you going to attack Netheril:** "Yes; I plan to attack and overthrow Netheril. The decadent humans of Netheril are controlled by wastrel archwizards whose greed is unequaled to anything else in the history of the world. Even the dragons, as they ruled the world millennia ago, never achieved this state of avarice. When Netheril falls, it shall be subjugated under my control, and the gluttony that threatens the nation's very existence will be put to death and Netheril will forever live."

• **Why do you hate Karsus:** "Karsus is the prime example of magical greed. His vices far exceeds any 10,000 people you can lump together. He's currently experimenting with magic far exceeding his power to control. Should he succeed, he will surely cause the whole nation to crumble and fall, killing everyone in his precious nation with a single breath."

• **Who are you:** "My name has been forgotten in history—I am the oldest living human in history. In lich form, I have lived thousands of years already—and I plan to live thousands more. Who better to rule a nation of magic than someone who's nearly seen the whole evolution of human magecraft? Even if I knew my real name, I could never tell you, for that would give you a certain amount of power over me."

If the characters do not attack the Lichlord, he finally grows bored with them and *teleports* them to the hill at the edge of the glade. If the characters attack and kill the Lichlord, his essence is transferred back to a specially prepared amulet deep below the castle. In a matter of minutes, the Lichlord has taken control of a Neth zombie and is using his special abilities to *teleport* the characters out of his castle to the hill where they met Amanda. Once *teleported*, the DM should refer to **The Army Moves** on page 51.

The Lichlord: AC –3; MV 9; HD 28; hp 196; THAC0 9; #AT 1; Dmg 1d10 (frigid touch); SA save vs. paralysis with touch or be unable to move until *dispelled*, creatures less than 5 HD must save vs. spell or flee in terror for 5d4 rounds, the Lichlord can unleash a *death ray* after enduring 50 points of magical damage that requires those within 20' to save vs. death or be permanently killed (once per day); SD at least +1 weapon or 6 HD (or levels) to hit, immune to *charm, sleep, enfeeblement, polymorph, cold, electricity, insanity,* or *death* spells; SW 13th-level priests and 15th-level paladins or greater can attempt to turn the lich as though they were five levels lower; SZ M (6' tall); ML fanatic (18); Int godlike (22); AL neutral evil; XP 10,000.

Notes: The Lichlord can see with normal vision even in complete darkness and is unaffected by bright light (even the magical variety). He radiates a 20'-radius aura of cold and darkness (darkness equivalent to dusk, even in magical *light*) forcing all his opponents to suffer a –2 on their Morale checks.

STR 13, DEX 13, CON 18, INT 22, WIS 19, CHA 1.

Personality: The Lichlord no longer carries any humanity (in the sense of sympathy and understanding) in his magically enhanced essence. He has one goal, and one goal only: to increase in power and knowledge at the expense of all—even at the expense of Prime Material existence.

The Lichlord has discovered that Karsus is working on a 12th-level spell—a height in magic he once thought impossible. Since a human arcanist is creating it and can't possibly understand the dangers involved, the Lichlord plans to take the information and, as a greater magical essence than any living being (especially Karsus of Netheril), study the incantation and use what he can of this new magical apex.

In order to achieve this goal, the Lichlord has erected his own *mythallar*, allowing him to control an army so huge and so terrifying, nothing of its ilk has ever been seen on the continent of Faerûn before. Once he recruits enough forces, the Lichlord plans to march them unceasingly through Netheril to the nearest Neth gatehouse and enter the Karsus Enclave. Once on the floating city, his forces will pour into the streets like rats from a drowning ship and take over every aspect of life there—including the position held by the Archwizard.

The Lichlord's clothing, surprisingly, has maintained its dweomer in spite of their outward appearance. (Strangely enough, the Lichlord's own dweomer has created the facade of decomposition and the putrefying rot in his clothing to make them "unfit" for human use.) The clothing has several very powerful dweomers cast upon it—all deactivated if the clothing isn't surrounding the body of a creature of unlife.

The known protection involved in the clothing include complete immunity to all elemental, quasielemental, and paraelemental forces; *Pockall's invisibility* to all magical scrying (a stronger form of the *nondetection* spell); the clothing creates a "one way mental mirror," allowing the Lichlord to use his mental powers, but reflecting all mental powers back at the source. The known offensive powers associated with the Lichlord's clothing include *spell reflection* of all spells 5th-level or less; 17 *Undine's extra portal pockets* in the clothing allow him to store a variety of wands, staves, and rods (which he does, but the actual number and the properties thereof change from day to day). There are no known weaknesses in the clothing.

The Lichlord can call upon any of the following spells. His spell book is hidden below the castle near his phylactery.

Spells (290/10): 1st—*Carbury's servant, General Matick's armor, General Matick's missile, General Matick's shield, Lefeber's mark, Niquie's reflection, Nobrow's fire effect, Quantoul's climber, Veridon's chiller, Veridon's wall, Yturn's feather fall, Zahn's familiar*; 2nd—*Aksa's shatter, Carbury's improved force, Carbury's mouth, Fahren's darkness, Jarm's summon swarm, Polybeus's illumination, Primidon's sphere, Ptack's knock, Ptack's locking, Quantoul's strength, Veridon's cloud, Yturn's levitation*; 3rd—*Aksa's object, Dace's tongue forms, dispel magic, Gwynn's vampirism, Hersent's sigil, Noanar's fireball, Quantoul's fastmorph, Quantoul's slowmorph, Quantoul's wraithmorph, Volhm's bolt*; 4th—*Carbury' killer, Fourfinger's enchanted weapon, Lefeber's first creation, Lucke's contagion, Noanar's trap, Noanar's wall, Quantoul's manymorph, Quantoul's othermorph, Quantoul's selfmorph, Xanad's shout*; 5th—*Jarm's magic jar, Lefeber's second creation, Oberon's telekinesis, Oberon's teleportation, Proctiv's rock-mud transformation, Shadow's demimonster, Shadow's door, Shadow's summons, Undine's avoidance, Zwei's second extension*; 6th—*Aksa's disintegrate, Carbury's stalker, Dethed's spell, Fourfinger's weather control, Lefeber's enchantment, Mavin's stone-flesh transformation, Tolodine's death fog, Volhm's chaining, Zwei's third extension*; 7th—*Dethed's death finger, Enollaf's isolation, Noanar's delayed fireball, Sadebreth's undead control, Shadow's walk, Trebbe's turning, Undine's door, Xanad's stun, Yong's dissipation*; 8th—*Aksa's morphing, Dethed's clone, Primidon's cloud, permanency, Toscudlo's dominance, Valdick's submerse, Xanad's blindness, Yong's truss*; 9th—*Anglin's sphere, Chronomancer's stasis, Chronomancer's time stop, Stoca's shapechange, Valdick's astral form, Valdick's gate, Volhm's drain, Xanad's killer*; 10th—*Lefeber's weave mythal, Mavin's create volcano, Mavin's earthfast, Proctiv's move mountain, Tolodine's killing wind, Valdick's spheresail.*

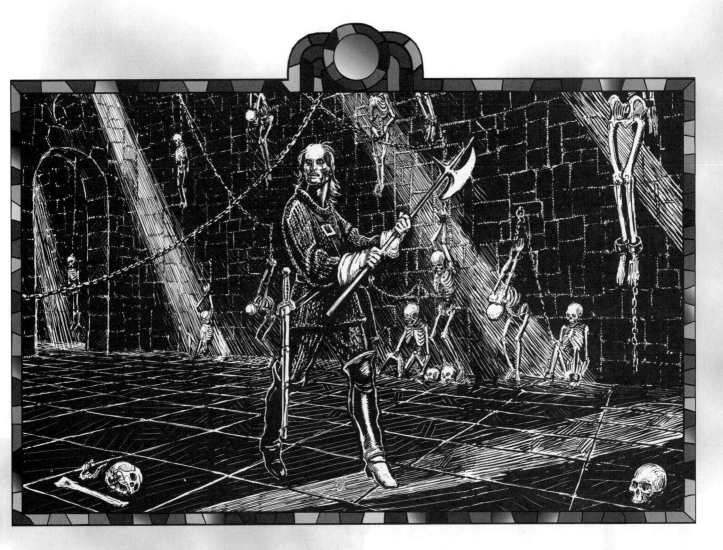

C. Cell, Occupied

These locations are jail cells that contain a prisoners that the Lichlord has not dealt with as of yet. The table below depicts who (or what) is in the cell.

Roll	Prisoner
1	**1d4 arcanists** (between 2nd and 8th level; roll 2d4). All are Netherese wizards who've come to destroy the Lichlord. Of good alignment, these wizards join the PCs if asked. There's a 25% chance per prisoner rescued that 1d12 zombies, wights, wraiths, or spectres (equal chance of each) appear and attack the PCs in order to prevent the prisoners from being freed.
2	**1d6 Angardt barbarians** (all warriors of 1d4 levels). They're kept here to test the vitality of the Angardt people. They're starved, skinny, and dirty, and have been given only water and a small amount of food to keep them alive. If the characters give them food to eat, the barbarians follow and obey the characters to the ends of Toril. There's a 10% chance per barbarian freed that 1d12 zombies attempt to stop them.
3	**Talin Crolas** (TN hm D17 [Jannath]) is sitting in here deciding his options after being captured earlier today. He's tried escaping a few times by changing into an earthworm and a snake, but he's been stopped each time by minions of the Lichlord. If released, Talin desires to leave the area as soon as possible to warn others of the Lichlord's army.
4	**1d4 Netherese fighters** of 3d4+4 levels reside in the cell. If freed, they'll help the characters. There's a 30% chance per warrior freed that 2d12 zombies attack.
5	**2d6 goblins.** The goblins have a Morale of 3, but they promise to help the PCs if they free them. The goblins must roll a Morale check with the first indication of battle. If it's failed, they flee in random directions, searching for a way out.
6	**1d8 orcs.** Even though they're of an evil alignment, the orcs will help the PCs destroy the Lichlord (they have a Morale of 10; roll this with the first Initiative roll). There's a 5% chance per freed orc that 1d8 zombies in the walls will attack.

D. Cell, Empty

Empty cells are difficult to spot within the castle; treat each of them as concealed doors. There's a 25% chance (rolled each time the party passes one of the doors to the empty cell) that the cell is actually occupied by one of the Lichlord's minions, who immediately attacks with a +2 bonus on its surprise roll if the PCs haven't discovered the door. The DM is free to select one of the creatures below or roll randomly.

Roll	Creature
1	**2d6 wraiths** (AC 4; MV 24, Fl 24 (B); HD 5+3; hp 30 each; THAC0 15; #AT 1; Dmg 1d6 + 1-level experience drain; SD can be struck only by magical weapons; SZ M (6' tall); ML champion (15); XP 2,000 each)
2	**1 ghost** (AC 0; MV 9; HD 10; hp 64; THAC0 11; #AT 1; Dmg age creatures 10–40 (1d4 × 10) years; SA *magic jar*, sight causes creature to age 10 years and flee for 2d6 turns unless a saving throw vs. spells is made; SD magical or silver weapons required to hit; SZ M (6' tall); ML n/a; XP 7,000).
3	**2d10 shadows** (AC 7; MV 12; HD 3+3; hp 21 each; THAC0 17; #AT 1; Dmg 1d4+1; SA Strength drain; SD magical weapons required to hit; SZ M (6' tall); ML n/a; XP 420 each).
4	**1–3 gray oozes** (AC 8; MV 1; HD 3+3; THAC0 17; #AT 1; Dmg 2d8; SA corrodes metal; SD immune to spells (except lightning); SZ L (10'); ML average (10); XP 270 each).

Each of these creatures passes through the walls to attack; they don't need to wait for the zombies to move to allow them to attack.

E. Mythallar

This room holds the Lichlord's *mythallar*. If the characters enter this room and stay longer than 10 seconds, the zombie walls and ceiling close in for the attack. Seventy zombies gain attacks from all sides and from the floor and ceiling, giving them at least four attacks per character. As zombies are destroyed by the PCs, others from different parts of the castle merge with the attackers, maintaining their overwhelming numbers. Meanwhile, the zombies form a wall between the characters and the *mythallar*, making sure they don't gain any opportunity to strike the *mythallar* at all. If

the PCs back out of the room the attacks stop. To destroy the *mythallar*, the characters must inflict 100 points of non-magical damage (all magical damage is absorbed).

F. Laboratory

This is the Lichlord's laboratory. It contains tables, cupboards, shelves, and a single chair made of living zombie bodies. Alchemical equipment, three traveling spell books (they contain the same spells as his master spell books hidden below the castle), and two vats of unholy water are all that remain in the chamber.

If characters investigate, they get the distinct impression that whatever magical research was being conducted here has recently been completed. A few experiments look like they've just begun, but it's hard to tell what their ultimate goal is supposed to be.

The Army Moves

From a distance, the castle fluidly collapses upon itself, spreading out onto the landscape like diseased mold. The *mythallar* can be clearly seen now that the walls of the undead have moved to the ground. Hundreds of zombielike beings reach down and hoist the blue, glowing ball upon their shoulders and begin to walk westward, following the line of death that stretches out like an asp ahead of it. Ninety or so of the undead climb upon each other, creating a pyramidal throne that looks like a giant siege machine; once constructed, the Lichlord blinks into existence atop their folded and stacked bodies, his glowing *mythallar* carried immediately behind him.

Thousands of these walking corpses head toward the fertile lands of Netheril, all intent upon murdering every living being they come across, converting them to unlife to strengthen their numbers.

The Conversion

No matter what direction they take or what they do, they have a run-in with Anointus. The first announcement of his arrival is a crossbow bolt from behind that causes 1d8 points of damage to one of the party's arcanists.

They see their old friend Anointus behind them, but there's something strange about him. As he approaches, they notice that he's dead; a former human converted to a Neth Zombie by the Lichlord's army.

Anointus, hm, Neth Zombie: AC –1; MV 12; F10; hp 57; THAC0 11; #AT 2; Dmg 1d8/1d8; MR 15%; SZ 6 1/2'; ML 20; AL N; XP 7,000.
Str 16, Dex 11, Con 13, Int 13, Wis 9, Cha 12.

Even in his undead form, he still maintains his pristine style. His clothes, boots, and equipment are in perfect order; his skin, on the other hand, is a different story. His blonde hair (at least the hair that hasn't rotted from his scalp) is perfectly styled, and his teeth are still pearly white, although the initial signs of his undeath are starting to shine through.

He arms himself with his polearm, *Separator*, and prepares for battle. "I've brought 57 people over to the Lichlord's side, and now it's your turn. I've been looking forward to this for many days now. Prepare to meet the bliss of rebirth." Anointus truly believes he's doing the characters a favor by converting them to unlife, and he's going to do his best to assure their alteration. Whenever a character falls in combat, he immediately uses his *raise dead* ability to bring defeated characters into the Lichlord's fold.

As the characters prepare to battle Anointus, they notice that the front ranks of the Lichlord's army have arrived. All characters are immediately faced with fighting creatures on every exposed front. Waves of undead (wights, wraiths, spectres, Neth zombies, and others) engulf the player-characters.

The PCs should feel like they're fighting for their life; that no matter how good they are or how many spells they have in their arsenal that it's just a matter of time before the undead overcome them. Keep track of hit points for the undead normally, but as one falls another immediately takes its place. During the battle—at its darkest moment—Karsus sends the characters a message.

Wrath of Karsus

Your minds fill with a vision of the Archwizard Karsus standing on a podium that overlooks his enclave. His voice fills your minds.

I have joined your battle. Prepare to see a sight so wondrous and joyous that your hearts will burst with pride!

The vision of Karsus begins to flicker and swell before your eyes, but you doubt the Archwizard has any idea what is happening to his body; his thoughts and energies are focused elsewhere. With a wave of his hand, the *mythallar* carried by the Lichlord's army explodes, sending a cascade of blue fire and ash everywhere.

As the Lichlord's source of power explodes, there is a numbing surge of electricity that sends chills down your spine. Your vision of Karsus suddenly winks out, and you hear the Archwizard's scream fill your minds.

If the characters are in hand-to-hand combat with the zombies, they are bathed in the intense heat. They must save vs. death magic or suffer a loss of 1d4 levels each. Whether they save or not, they suffer 4d6 points of magical fire damage.

At this point, all magic upon Faerûn ceases to exist. Spells wink out, magical items lose their enchantments, and quasimagical items are rendered forever inert. Even creatures that normally require magical weapons to be hit are affected by normal weapons.

When the cascade of blue fire clears, the players see that all of the undead have been turned to ash—except the Lichlord. Stumbling through the landscape in a daze, the Lichlord begins to run away from the heroes.

The Lichlord has lost half of his hit points and can only move half as fast as human (Movement Rate 6) under the best circumstances. Without his spells and magical abilities to help him, he has more to lose than to gain by challenging the player-characters. And if he dies now, his phylactery won't do him any good (his spirit won't be able to go from his ruined form to another; he'll be dead forever).

For the next five rounds, the player-characters have a chance to destroy the Lichlord forever. It's going to be a straight melee combat, with the Lichlord reduced to striking physically with his bone-chilling touch (which still works because his tie to the Negative Material Plane remains intact). If the Lichlord survives for five rounds, he regains the use of his spells and *fear* aura and *teleports* away at the earliest possible opportunity.

Epilogue

With the heroes standing among the charred ashes of the Lichlord's army, a great calm descends over the battlefield. Everyone gets the feeling that something significant has just happened. Priests lose contact with their gods, all spellcasting is impossible, and quasimagical items are rendered inert. Character abilities are likewise altered.

Classes

From the moment Netheril falls, the rules that allowed Netheril to rise to such fantastic heights are changed forever. For spellcasting classes, these changes are viewed as catastrophic.

			Druid Spells by Level				
X.P.	Level	Level Title	1	2	3	4	5
0	1	Rhymer	1	—	—	—	—
2,001	2	Lyrist	2	—	—	—	—
4,001	3	Sonnateer	3	—	—	—	—
8,001	4	Skald	3	1	—	—	—
16,001	5	Racaraide	3	2	—	—	—
25,001	6	Joungleur	3	3	—	—	—
40,001	7	Troubador	3	3	1	—	—
60,001	8	Minstrel	3	3	2	—	—
85,001	9	Muse	3	3	3	—	—
110,001	10	Lorist	3	3	3	1	—
150,001	11	Bard	3	3	3	2	—
200,001	12	Master Bard	3	3	3	3	—
400,001	13	Master Bard	3	3	3	3	1
600,001	14	Master Bard	3	3	3	3	2
800,001	15	Master Bard	3	3	3	3	3
1,000,001	16	Master Bard	4	3	3	3	3
1,200,001	17	Master Bard	4	4	3	3	3
1,400,001	18	Master Bard	4	4	4	3	3
1,600,001	19	Master Bard	4	4	4	4	3
1,800,001	20	Master Bard	5	4	4	4	4
2,000,001	21	Master Bard	5	5	4	4	4
2,200,001	22	Master Bard	5	5	5	4	4
3,000,001+	23	Master Bard	5	5	5	5	5

Bard Colleges & Abilities Table

Bard Level	College	Additional Languages	Charm Percentage	Legend Lore
1	None (Probationer)	—	15%	0%
2	Fochlucan	—	20%	5%
3	Fochlucan	—	22%	7%
4	Fochlucan	1	24%	10%
5	Mac-Fuirmidh	—	30%	13%
6	Mac-Fuirmidh	1	32%	16%
7	Mac-Fuirmidh	—	34%	20%
8	Doss	—	40%	25%
9	Doss	1	42%	30%
10	Doss	1	44%	35%
11	Canaith	—	50%	40%
12	Canaith	1	53%	45%
13	Canaith	1	56%	50%
14	Cli	—	60%	55%
15	Cli	1	63%	60%
16	Cli	1	66%	65%
17	Anstruth	—	70%	70%
18	Anstruth	1	73%	75%
19	Anstruth	1	76%	80%
20	Ollamh	1	80%	85%
21	Ollamh	1	84%	90%
22	Ollamh	1	88%	95%
23	Magna Alumnae	1	95%	99%

For DMs who desire to be historically accurate, game play reverts to strict original AD&D rules (not 2nd Edition). This means that clerics and druids are two separate classes, as are mages and illusionists. Specialty priests and specialist wizards no longer exist. Cantras are no longer available to the everyday folk.

Arcanists

Those most responsible for the Fall are stripped of spell-casting ability until they figure out how the Weave works again. This time period is a base of 30 days, modified by their Intelligence score. Thus, an arcanist with 18 Intelligence requires 12 days of hard work to figure out how the weave has been changed by Mystra.

During this time, the arcanist struggles to rework his spell book, memorize the arcane runes required to cast spells, and generally re-orient himself with the magical world around him.

Arcanists also change the name of their profession to match that of the elves, and they begin calling themselves mages. This was brought about by the intense hatred many arcanists faced after the Fall by those who blamed them for the catastrophe.

Arcanists now use the spell memorization tables as listed in the *Player's Handbook*. While there are still no damage caps on spells, 10th-level and higher magic no longer exists. Arcanist spells merge together to become mage spells; specialization in a particular school of magic doesn't exist until the Time of Troubles.

Priests

Priests immediately lose all of their special abilities, the gods having removed specialty priests' granted powers. Until the Time of Troubles, only clerics and druids walk the land (though specialty priests begin to emerge about 30 years before that time). Quest spells are likewise stripped from priests.

The priests of former Netheril begin to pray for spells each morning, but the lengthy relearning process that arcanists face requires but a single week for priests, who are guided by their god. After that week, clerics of Netheril discover that they have access to only the Transcendent Winds; druids have access to only the Terrestrial Winds. Clerics and druids advance as detailed in the *Player's Handbook*, memorizing spells and gairing bonus spells for high Wisdom as detailed.

The priests of Netheril are the ones responsible for telling the people the truth behind what happened to the empire. While the arcanists tried to hide from the public view, priests were there to tend to the survivors both physically and emotionally. The dedication of the priests paid off in terms of magnificent temples and a healthy following for their gods.

Rogues

Thieves mostly celebrated after the Fall, grateful that the powerful archwizards had been removed from power. They migrated south with the other survivors, blending into the new civilizations that formed in the wake of Netheril.

Of course, there were a great many enemies that survived the Fall, and assassins were hired from the ranks of the thieves' guilds to perform these dark deeds. Soon, the assassins had a guild of their own.

The reformation of the bards after the Fall of Netheril nearly destroyed the profession. Bards left their dependence on wizard spells behind, instead opting to learn a bit about everything. They became fighters (until 5th level or so) and then became thieves, remaining so until they had achieved at least 5th level in their new class. Finally, they left thievery behind to study with the druids, gaining druid spells as they advanced.

Player-character bards who survived the Fall advance as detailed below, but they gain druid spells instead of mage spells.

Bards begin as Rhymers, but they don't gain any hit points for achieving first level. Instead, they use the hit points they acquired as a fighter and thief. Upon achieving 2nd level, bards get to roll a single six-sided die for hit points. After achieving 10th level as a bard, they gain one hit point per level.

Bards also belonged to colleges based on their level. These colleges served as a matter of great personal achievement for a bard, and they hardly ever associated with bards of a lesser college. The exception to this rule were the *Magna Alumnae* bards, who freely offered advice and suggestions to bards of all levels and colleges.

Bards also gained the ability to cast a *charm person* or *charm monster* spell through music. Saving throws apply (as does magic resistance).

As students of the world, bards learned many languages. Their travels frequently brought them into contact with many races and different cultures, and those that learned new languages brought back the information and passed it along to others. As a bard advanced in level, he learned these languages.

The final ability that bards gained was *legend lore*, the ability to know something about an item from merely handling it. This worked exactly like the wizard spell of the same name.

The chart below details the colleges, charm percentage, bonus languages, and *legend lore* percent as the bard advances in level.

Warriors

Fighters, rangers, and paladins were mostly responsible for Netheril's survival. Gathering the people together, these brave souls led them through the Wildlands to the more tame lands of the south. Still, rangers and paladins were affected by the restructuring of magic.

Paladins benefited a great deal from the change in magic, being allowed to cast any cleric (Transcendent Wind) spell available to them after they achieved 9th level. Like clerics, they were required to pray each morning to have their spells bestowed to them.

Ranger Spell Progression

Paladin Level	Casting Level	Clerical Spell Level			
		1	2	3	4
9	1	1	—	—	—
10	2	2	—	—	—
11	3	2	1	—	—
12	4	2	2	—	—
13	5	2	2	1	—
14	6	3	2	1	—
15	7	3	2	1	1
16	8	3	3	1	1
17	9	3	3	2	1
18	10	3	3	3	1
19	11	3	3	3	2
20*	12	3	3	3	3

* Maximum spell ability

Rangers branched out from their normal activities as well, casting both druid and mage spells as they advanced in level. While they had to pray for their druid spells each morning, magic-user spells had to be discovered and then memorized (they were not granted by their god). Rangers gain spells as detailed below.

One of the biggest advantages that rangers received after the Fall is that they gained a +1 damage adjustment versus all giant-class monsters (giants, bugbears, ettins, gnolls, goblins, and others) for each level of experience.

Paladin Spell Table

Paladin Level	Casting Level	Clerical Spell Level			
		1	2	3	4
9	1	1	—	—	—
10	2	2	—	—	—
11	3	2	1	—	—
12	4	2	2	—	—
13	5	2	2	1	—
14	6	3	2	1	—
15	7	3	2	1	1
16	8	3	3	1	1
17	9	3	3	2	1
18	10	3	3	3	1
19	11	3	3	3	2
20*	12	3	3	3	3

* Maximum spell ability

Spell Names

Mages quickly tried to forget about the arcanists of Netheril, dropping their names from spells and magical items. *Noanar's fireball* became known simply as *fireball*, and other name spells suffered a similar fate. This made room for a new class of mages to make their mark upon the world, including such notables as Tenser, Bigby, Elminster, the Simbul, Khelben, Mordenkainen, and others.

Where to?

Where the player-characters go from here is largely a matter of personal preference. If they travel north into the heart of the empire, they run across battered refugees fleeing south. Many of the survivors are running from bloodthirsty tribes of orcs that are preying upon them during their flight.

To the east, the elves of Cormanthyr offer a brief, unwelcome refuge for the survivors. Arcanists unknown to the elves receive a bitterly cold welcome (with some downright hostility in some cases), while those who are friends of the elves are received slightly better. After all, the elves aren't happy about the changes brought about by Karsus's arrogance either.

West of Netheril is the Savage Frontier. Some floating cities, which never really considered themselves part of the empire, fell to the ground there as well. Many of the survivors chose to build small communities instead of migrate with the other Netherese survivors.

Since the player-characters are already in the south, waiting for survivors to arrive takes around two weeks. From there, the survivors split to form the countries of Anauria, Asram, and Hlondath. Of course, it will take strong leaders to bring the people together again (and those nations have their own fates that a wise and just ruler has to deal with).

At the end of this adventure are a variety of rumors and adventure hooks that the DM can integrate into a post-Netheril campaign. Use the ones that suit your specific vision of Netheril and discard the rest. If the PCs are time travelers, they need only survive until the beginning of the year to be whisked through the *time conduit* to present-day Faerûn.

With the fall of Netheril, one can only blame the Netherese fate upon themselves. Decadent and completely reliant on magic and spellcraft, the refugees of the crumbled empire scatter to the four corners of the world, hoping to find some vista of safety from the threats of the real world around them—the threats they've been able to ignore for many millennia because of the power and might of their archwizard leaders. Their dependence on their spellcasting leaders have led them to a form of retardation; survival techniques and ways to handle the threats their ancestors dealt with on a daily basis are sadly lacking. It's surprising to historians that the Netheril survivors were able to endure at all.

Netheril as a civilization has left its mark on the world. Its magic, the height of its spellcasters, and the discoveries made throughout the planes are unparalleled. Only in the future do humans regain their mastery of magic. In this far future, humankind looks back on Netheril's reign with awe and pride, mostly due to the cloudy stories and songs of legend.

SPELLS & MAGIC

Hundreds — even thousands — of magical items and spells exist in Netheril, and few of those creations survived the Fall. In addition to those described in the Empire of Magic boxed set, the following spells and magical items made their mark in some small way in Netheril.

New Spell

As terrifying and powerful as high-level spells are, much of the true research in spellcasting occurs at lower levels, at a depth in the weave that a common spellcaster can achieve. These are also the spells that the common people talked about with more spirit, having witnessed their effects from time to time in arenas, schools of magic, or happenstance.

Chevic's Tracer

(Divination/Alteration)
Level: 4
Field: Mentalism
Range: Touch
Components: V, M
Duration: Permanent
Casting Time: 7
Area of Effect: One Person
Saving Throw: Neg.

The *tracer* spell was designed by a bounty-hunting arcanist who was tired of running into a mark and having them escape at the last second, only to have to hunt them down again. The spell he designed allowed him to spot a target and place a dweomer on the victim. Once the *tracer* was set, Chevic was able to *teleport* to within 10 feet of the victim in order to try and bring the criminal in to face justice.

Up to one *tracer* can be placed on victim for every five levels of the spell caster. By simply willing it, the arcanist is able to "break" the tracer, freeing up a spell for yet another bounty target. The spell requires vocal components as well as a cube of lodestone.

New Equipment

A few pieces of equipment in the adventure are one-of-a-kind items, while the remaining were known to be in wide use throughout Netheril. Unless otherwise noted in the item's description, all of these magical items operated at 12th level of ability.

Consumption Armor

This armor can be of any type, from plate to leather. When it's used in defense against normal, nonmagical attacks, treat *consumption armor* as normal armor. When it defends against magical attacks, however, its true nature becomes apparent.

When a magical attack strikes the user of this armor, the armor gains the ability to ward later damage. For each level of spell cast at the wearer, the armor stores one point of physical damage. The user still suffers normal damage from the magical attack, however (standard saving throws apply).

For instance, a *Noanar's fireball* cast at the user of the armor stores three hit points of damage. If an orc later causes 5 hit points of damage with a club, the damage is reduced to 2 hit points. If only 2 hit points of damage was inflicted, the wearer wouldn't suffer any damage.

The amount of damage that *consumption armor* can absorb and the length of time that the damage can be "stored" is based upon the level of its creator. Armor can absorb up to one points' worth of damage per level of its creator, holding it for a number of days equal to one-third its creator's level. Some commonly found sets of armor appear below:

% Roll	Armor Type	Absorption Points	Storage Time
01–20	*Banded mail +2*	15	5 days
21–30	*Leather +3*	15	5 days
31–35	*Chain mail +3*	18	6 days
36–42	*Plate mail +1*	20	6 days
43–45	*Plate mail +3*	24	8 days
46–52	*Scale mail +2*	15	5 days
52–60	*Ring mail +2*	15	5 days
61–70	*Leather +4*	24	8 days
71–77	*Studded leather +3*	15	5 days
78–85	*Banded mail +3*	21	7 days
86–92	*Scale mail +3*	21	7 days
93–97	*Chain mail +4*	24	8 days
98–99	*Any available +4*	21	7 days
00	*Plate mail +5*	40	13 days

Once the armor's absorption capabilities are reached, it affords its wearer no further protection.

Deflector

Anointus's shield, *Deflector*, is a beautifully restored body shield from the earliest days of Netheril. Many antique dealers believe the shield was forged in the year 14 NY, but art and weapon collectors believe the date to be about 20 years later.

Deflector has a small engraving on its lowest point showing a symbol of a hammer crossed with a sword, believed to be the sigil of the master craftsman Yryic Friothyn. Most historians agree that the shield was probably never held by Nether the Elder himself, but by his son, Nether the Young.

Deflector is the envy of many art, antique, and weapon collectors. Its surface is engraved with the original sigil of Nether the Elder, the first king of Netheril. It's believed by scholars and collectors alike that Nether the Young commissioned the work to have something to instill pride in his warriors during time of battle.

Deflector has a time-looping effect on it that constantly returns the shield to its original condition and look. No amount of tampering, hammering, or slicing has a permanent effect. Within minutes, any gems, studded emblems, or melee-induced marring disappears, and the original surface shines through.

Due to its incredible history, the shield is a heavily sought-after item. Many collectors have sent scores of mercenaries looking for *Deflector*, and many have succeeded. At least 17 collectors (and their heirs) have held the shield in their collections, only to be stolen by lecherous peddlers and craven warriors (usually at the expense of the previous owner's life). Anointus gained ownership of the shield when he was on his first adventuring tour with his father, who was a prized ranger in Ioulaum's court. His father was commissioned by the Father of Netheril to take a group of businessmen who desired a prized piece of property in Ioulaum.

Where *Deflector* ended up after the fall of Netheril is unknown. Anointus was killed shortly before the Fall, and the whereabouts of all his gear is unknown. It's believed that someone near him, perhaps a traveling companion, took all of his equipment and either claimed the items as his own or buried them in a safe place for later extraction. For centuries, many adventurers and hired explorers were commissioned for unbelievable sums of money to find the equipment and return them to the survivor state of Hlondath, but nothing was ever discovered. The only thing they found was a lone tombstone close to the Eastern Forest's former western borders (which by that time had receded to nearly nothing).

Dr. Killdrum's Wand of Fireballs

A variation of the *wand of fireballs*, this wand is set under the skin and bone of the right arm. Unlike other wands, the strength of the enchantment is under the direct control of the owner.

Its owner must expend part of his life force (in the form of hit points) to power the wand. For every hit point expended in "charging" the wand, the creates a one-die *Noanar's fireball*. The only limit known for this is the number of available hit points in the owner's body. For instance, Dr. Killdrum has 45 hit points, so he could create a 44d6 *Noanar's fireball*, rendering him nearly dead (only one hit point remaining).

An interesting side effect has been discovered through adventuring and other unfortunate incidents—Dr. Killdrum and his gear have become immune to magical and natural fire.

For the *wand of fireballs* to be implanted, the recipient suffers a total of 20 hit points of damage and loses the use of the arm for 20 weeks (subtract the recipient's Constitution from the debilitative time period). Until this time for healing is complete, the *wand* cannot be used.

Dying Woman's Leather Ensemble

This unknown woman had one of the most powerful leather armor outfits created in Netheril's history. A real magical item (as opposed to a quasimagical device), the leather can function outside the area of effect of a *mythallar*.

Paranoid of a dream she suffered as a young girl, this woman had a fancy black leather suit of armor enchanted to protect her from all the elemental forces known to Netheril, including paraelemental and quasielemental forces. The leather, in spite of its use and age, looks brand new (probably a side effect from the elemental protection magic instilled into the leather). The leather protects the user from the following effects, including attacks from elementals of the stated kind:

• **Elemental:** air, earth, fire, and water (including magical waters and water-based potions and poisons).

• **Paraelemental:** ice (and ice- and cold-based spells), magma, ooze, and smoke (including smoke spells and items).

• **Quasielemental:** ash, dust (including magical dusts), lightning (magical and mundane), minerals, radiance (including all *light* spells), salt, steam, and vacuum.

Edie's Cloak

A gift from Edie's teacher, Ioulaum, this cloak was a magical item that continued to gain power as it aged. When she first received it, the magic in the cloak was a simple *cloak of displacement*. Since its creation, Edie's cloak has gained the following powers:

• Acts as a *ring of spell storing*

• It has seven permanent *Undine's extra portal pockets* scattered throughout the inside of the cloak.

• It acts as an *elemental compass*

• The wearer is rendered *invisible* to those who are *invisible*, *displaced*, or *planar* (ethereal and astral).

• Twelve weapons of small size, six medium weapons, four large weapons, or any combination thereof, can be hidden away in the sleeves of the cloak. (Use the following guide to determine if there's room in the cloak: 1 large=3 small; 1 medium=2 small.) All hidden objects cannot be discovered by a casual search.

• Acts as a *lens of charming*

• Whenever death magic (magic that could cause instant death) is used against the wearer, there's a chance that an ability score is raised (assuming the wearer survives the death magic attack). Roll 1d6 to determine which ability is affected (1=Cha, 2=Con, 3=Dex, 4=Int, 5=Str, and 6=Wis). Once the ability is determined, the wearer must roll a 1d20 against the ability score. If the die roll is *greater* than the ability score, the score is raised one point. (No score can be raised above 19 in this manner.)

Floating Bubble

Floating bubbles are a common way to transfer objects or living beings from one location to another. When they were originally made, each one, depending upon the purpose it served, had a different opaque color. For instance, chocolate *floating bubbles* carried precious cargo, and both fuchsia and walnut held animals. When thieves discovered the color schemes, they took advantage of this knowledge and often chased the bubbles down—often for hours—in order to capture the cargo (or release it in the case of transported prisoners). *Floating bubbles* alter their size to the cargo they carry (they're all perfectly spherical).

When thieves began stealing transit cargo, the *bubbles* were improved, given better speed and evasive capabilities (all this is taken into account with Movement Rates, Hit Points, and Armor Class).

The first table below depicts the original meaning of the colors. This information, however, is effectively useless after 2107 NY when the color scheme was given up and random colors attached to each *bubble*.

The second table shows the changes and improvements made on the *floating bubbles* throughout Netheril's history. This information should be given to players using characters created specifically for the Netheril setting.

1d8	Color	Purpose
1	Almond	Personnel transportation
2	Chocolate	Precious cargo
3	Cobalt	Nonperishable products
4	Ebony	Prisoners
5	Fuchsia	Animals (horses)
6	Iris	Perishable products
7	Raspberry	Nonprecious cargoes
8	Walnut	Animals (food)

Year (NY)	HP	AC	Special
2068-2107	5	7	MV 12; Moves directly toward target.
2108-2574	15	7	MV 12; +1 AC bonus vs. bludgeoning.
2575-2980	30	5	MV 15; +2 AC bonus vs. bludgeoning; +1 vs. spell saves.
2981-3166	50	4	MV 18; +2 AC bonus vs. bludgeoning; +1 AC vs. slashing and stabbing weapons; +2 vs. spell and rod/staff/wand saves.
3167-3520	75	3	MV 21; immune to nonmagical attacks; +3 bonus vs. all magic-related saving throws.

Krystaufer's Spell Book

Krystaufer's amazing spell book is a small notebook-sized booklet measuring one-half inch thick, two inches wide, and three inches tall. However, when the cover is lifted to reveal the pages within, the book instantly expands to 12-times its size, rendering the above dimensions in feet (instead of inches), allowing the user to easily read the pages. When the covers are closed, it shrinks back to its original size.

The spells found in this tome are: *Berthot's blunder*, *Berthot's disorder*, *Cragh's deafness*, *Enollaf's aimlessness*, *Hamring's enfeeblement*, *Hamring's feeblemind*, *Keonid's charm human*, *Keonid's fear*, *Keonid's forgetfulness*, *Keonid's suggestion*, *M'dhal's missile shield*, *M'dhal's remove evil II*, *Oberon's extradoor*, *Prug's dominate*, *Quantoul's changer*, *Smolyn's blindness*, *Smolyn's eyebite*, *Trebbe's invulnerability*, *Trebbe's minor invulnerability*, *Trebbe's scry identify*, *Trebbe's scry magic*, *Trebbe's turning*, *Undine's avoidance*, *Zahn's hearing*, and *Zahn's seeing*.

On the last seven pages of *Krystaufer's spell book*, he keeps careful notes on 17 poisons of his own, personal concoction. These powerful brews often put alchemical professionals to shame, raising his fame among thieves and assassins. Most of the mixtures are two and three stage poisons, with one four-part poison that's hard to manage and, more often than not, fails. An alchemy background (in the form of the healing and/or herbalism nonweapon proficiency) is necessary to produce results, though success is not guaranteed. Without this ability, the user simply must roll an Intelligence check at one-half in order to achieve the desired results from the poison.

Poison	Method	Onset	Fail	Save
312.3512	contact	1d3 hrs	Debil	20
Adelaine's	ingest	2d6 hrs	2d10	1d10
Causkrys	contact	1d4 min	2d8	2d4
Centipoison	inject	2d6 min	Debil	30
Delabonna	ingest	1d4 hrs	20	10
Evileac	contact	2d12 hrs	Paraly	Debil
K-Juice	inject	Immediate	Death	20
Krysalis	inject	1d4+1 min	25	10
Mercurine	ingest	2d6 min	50	25
Number 17	contact	2d4 min	Para	Nil
Paralye	contact	1 min	Death	25
Plaguerrilla	inject	10d3 min	Debil	Nil
Primer, The	contact	2 min	Death	30
Taintake	inject	Immediate	Death	15
Toxingest	ingest	1d4 min	Death	20
Venom 12c	contact	2d4 min	Paraly	Debil
X-Venom	inject	1d2 min	40	2d12

Lichlord's Spell Book

The *Lichlord's spell book* is one of the biggest tomes dedicated to the ways of magic that can be found in Netheril. The covers are dried and preserved maple wrapped in the skin of a Shadowtop Clan member, showing his contempt for the elven race.

The spell book's pages are pounded and dried ogre tripe discolored to a mute beige with the use of bleaches and lye. In spite of their construction matter and the fact that the book is at least a millennia old, the pages are pliable and bend with turning. An old ink recipe borrowed from the *nether scrolls* allows only the undead to read the magical concoction written on the pages. Even a *read magic* doesn't reveal the spells. (Casting *read magic*, *comprehend languages*, and *vampiric touch* allows a living creature to be able to read the spells.)

The Lichlord's spell book contains an extensive interpretation of the necromantic sections of the *nether scrolls* (incomplete, since there were subjects within the scrolls that the Lichlord had not yet mastered). His spells include:

1st—Carbury's servant, General Matick's armor, General Matick's missile, General Matick's shield, Lefeber's mark, Niquie's reflection, Nobrow's fire effect, Quantoul's climber, Veridon's chiller, Veridon's wall, Yturn's feather fall, Zahn's familiar; 2nd—Aksa's shatter, Carbury's improved force, Carbury's mouth, Fahren's darkness, Jarm's summon swarm, Polybeus's illumination, Primidon's sphere, Ptack's knock, Ptack's locking, Quantoul's strength, Veridon's cloud, Yturn's levitation; 3rd—Aksa's object, Dace's tongue forms, dispel magic, Gwynn's vampirism, Hersent's sigil, Noanar's fireball, Quantoul's fastmorph, Quantoul's slowmorph, Quantoul's wraithmorph, Volhm's bolt; 4th—Carbury' killer, Fourfinger's enchanted weapon, Lefeber's first creation, Lucke's contagion, Noanar's trap, Noanar's wall, Quantoul's manymorph, Quantoul's othermorph, Quantoul's selfmorph, Xanad's shout; 5th—Jarm's magic jar, Lefeber's second creation, Oberon's telekinesis, Oberon's teleportation, Proctiv's rock-mud transformation, Shadow's demimonster, Shadow's door, Shadow's summons, Undine's avoidance, Zwei's second extension; 6th—Aksa's disintegrate, Carbury's stalker, Dethed's spell, Fourfinger's weather control, Lefeber's enchantment, Mavin's stone-flesh transformation, Tolodine's death fog, Volhm's chaining, Zwei's third extension; 7th—Dethed's death finger, Enollaf's isolation,

Noanar's delayed fireball, Sadebreth's undead control, Shadow's walk, Trebbe's turning, Undine's door, Xanad's stun, Yong's dissipation; 8th—Aksa's morphing, Dethed's clone, Primidon's cloud, permanency, Toscudlo's dominance, Valdick's submerse, Xanad's blindness, Yong's truss; 9th—Anglin's sphere, Chronomancer's stasis, Chronomancer's time stop, Stoca's shapechange, Valdick's astral form, Valdick's gate, Volhm's drain, Xanad's killer; 10th—Lefeber's weave mythal, Mavin's create volcano, Mavin's earthfast, Proctiv's move mountain, Tolodine's killing wind, Valdick's spheresail.

Neth Tattoo

Designed in 3150 NY and perfected in 3490 NY, the *Neth tattoo* is a magically inscribed drawing. Usually placed on the forearms or the exposed flesh of the neck, chest, or legs, the *tattoo* is designed to release a magical effect at the will of the wearer. Only a few documented instances show the use of a *Neth tattoo*, so the complete process is a relatively secretive one, though it's known that several archwizards and many other high-level arcanists (as well as their trusted friends) used them.

When a *Neth tattoo* is placed on the skin, it takes the form of a moving shape desired by the recipient. Often, the shape seems bathed in mist, making it appear as a noncorporeal silhouette. As the *tattoo* is inscribed, additional spellcasting is done in order to give the tattoo "life" and power; any arcanist spell can be inlaid into the tattoo. To release the spell effect, the recipient simply activates it by mental command, and "points" at a target with his eyes.

Up to one *Neth tattoo* can be safely placed on a body per two points of Constitution. The magic that's inherently active in the *tattoo* can cause great physical stress should more be attempted, requiring a Constitution check (modified as a penalty by the number of *tattoos* placed on the body). If this check fails, the spell effect contained in the *Neth tattoo* is immediately released.

• *Skull of Quietusmagia:* This is a protective enchantment that disables magic that touches the flesh (or enters the body) of the one emblazoned with this *Neth tattoo*. For instance, enchanted weapons (blessed or cursed) lose their bonuses when used against one with this tattoo. Personal-effect spells and effects are rendered impotent against the character possessing this rune. Each *quietusmagia* tattoo placed on the body renders the character immune to magic for one hour. The tattoo is activated when the wearer is attacked by a magic effect, and the one-hour-long protection begins at that time. If more than one *quietusmagia* is tattooed on the body, only one activates at a time. Note that magical healing, *invisibility*, and similar effects aren't possible while protected by this rune, so its ownership is somewhat of a mixed blessing.

Any tattoo placed on a creature exacts its price, however, permanently reducing that creature's Constitution score by one. The procedure for placing a tattoo requires 1d4 hours plus one hour per spell level.

Protector

Anointus's armor, *protector*, is a fantastic piece of work, though it does show the age of centuries (either that or the short lives of its previous owners) upon its surface. The armor is constructed of a refractive, blue metal that splits white light into its separate colors (resembling rainbows). Forged by a craftswoman in Yeoman's Loft, the artisan refused to tell Anointus what metal was used in the armor, and no manner of convincing, bribery, or magical augury would pull the information out of the woman's brain.

The armor renders the wearer immune to all *light* spells and spells that use light as an attack form. The armor renders the user *invisible* to other planar sources and creatures (the user is invisible to ethereal, *gated*, conjured, and planar beings, for example).

The armor also grants a certain immunity to weapons, for the wearer's opponents find their target a bit harder to strike than one would seem (granting a +4 Armor Class bonus). Along with this bonus, the armor removes one hit point of damage from each and every blow against the wearer, with a minimum amount of one point of damage.

Separator

Anointus's weapon is an axe-headed polearm standing 6 ½' in length. The head is forged from pure adamantine, given to him as a gift from the dwarves at Delzoun in appreciation for his work in an assault by fiends in the year 3500 NY. Enchanted by an archwizard (some believe this friend was none other than Lady Polaris herself), it's a true magical item, as opposed to being quasimagically bewitched. Being a +2/+3/+5 weapon, the polearm grants a +5 attack and damage bonus vs. *gated* or summoned creatures, +3 vs. evilly aligned targets, and +2 vs. all other nongood targets.

The polearm is not intelligent, but it possesses the ability to perceive the emotions of the wielder (used to prepare itself), granting the possessor a +2 Initiative modifier in the first round of combat (so long as the opponent is nongood). By mental command, while the shaft of the weapon is in direct contact with skin, the wielder can have *Separator* empathically perceive the emotions of any one target and transmit the results to the owner. Only one target can be chosen in any round, and only five such readings can be done in an hour's time.

Twinrazor

This is a *+3 bastard sword* that can easily be wielded one handed due to its near-weightless properties. When the sword is brandished before a battle and before it draws its first blood, it leaves long, drawn-out traces of light and releases a terrifying tone requiring all who oppose the wielder to make a saving throw vs. spell or run in *fear* for 1d4+2 rounds.

Twinrazor has the following additional powers: it allows the wielder to attack first in every round (as a *scimitar of speed*) and allows the wielder to call upon a *haste* spell once per day.

Warmthstone

The *warmthstone* is a three-inch-diameter rock created by an unknown arcanist about 150 years before the Fall. The *warmthstone* creates the heat of a medium-sized campfire when activated by voice command for as long as it's in use. It creates no light, though *infravision* detects the rock's presence. When deactivated, the stone immediately disperses all of its heat and its owner can safely pick it up and place it in a pack. The stone weights three pounds, comes in any natural stone color, and is generally flat on one end to keep the *warmthstone* from rolling about.

Rumors & Hooks

ere's a list of rumors and myths the Dungeon Master can throw into the mix in order to increase the adventuring potential for the Netheril boxed set.

☞ The characters' experiences in Netheril are only illusions created by the venom of a poisoned arrow fired by the heroes' last opponent before their entrance into Netheril. If the DM wants this rumor to be true, this is an easy way for him to bring the characters back to their normal time without any trouble whatsoever. All they've got to do is wait for the toxins to wear off.

While unconscious in this manner, time does not necessarily flow at the same rate. This means a whole month could pass in their tainted dreams while only moments have passed in real time. If the DM decides to use this as a campaign escape route, he should create some doubt. This can be done by allowing the characters to keep one item (magical or not) from their time in Netheril in order to make them wonder if it was truly a delusion brought on by poison!

☞ Karsus is really a frail yet shockingly beautiful woman disguised to look like a man in order to appear fearsome. This poses an interesting situation. Is Karsus really an archwizard, or is he/she nothing more than a puppet for a greater being who shuns the limelight, manipulating events from the backstage?

☞ The Lichlord is a time-traveling personality from the future who wants only to capture enough magic from Netheril to facilitate his return through 7,000 years of history. He's not going to let anything stand in his way.

☞ The Abbey of the Moon has rebuilt itself. Sages from Karsus Enclave believe that the Abbey has somehow absorbed the personalities of the apparitions who have been haunting its charred halls. Apparently a dozen human monks (ranging in age from 12 to 106) are planning to make a walking pilgrimage to the old holy site in order to take up residence there. They're looking for guides and guards for this long, five-month journey.

☞ An adventurer has found the *nether scrolls*. The explorer is returning to Holloway to put the scrolls up for public auction, where she hopes to gain a tremendous amount of money for them. She's invited Cormanthyr elves, the phaerimm, and high-profile Netherese to the auction to create the biggest bidding war in history.

☞ The phaerimm have taken notice of the player-characters and have sent six assassins to eliminate this new threat. The assassins, Netherese warriors and arcanists from the city of Gers, have placed a *tracer* on the characters in order to maintain vigilant surveillance.

☞ Ioulaum, the arcanist who created the first flying city, is really a lizardman who resides in a swamp somewhere in Neth Central (the central portion of Netheril). He's trying to remove all the other archwizards in order to gain control of the whole nation. Once he's entrenched in power, he plans to outlaw further magical research, beginning with the murder of every theoretical alchemist and magical savant he can lay his hands on.

☞ Adrian Freeman is under the complete control of phaerimm who are attempting to bring the magical nation of Netheril down from the inside through corruption and high-level spell research. Illithids are keeping a close synapse on Adrian, alerting the phaerimm should anyone discover his little secret. The phaerimm will undoubtedly save Adrian's life at the expense of those who should attempt to kill him.

☞ Tanar'ri are humans who were evil in their living days, and their essences were altered "physically" to match the ugliness that stained their souls. Enough *bless* spells cast on the tanar'ri causes the poor creature to revert to goodness. Then, and only then, the essence of the former evil human can rest in peace.

☞ The illithid and the phaerimm are working together to bring down the Netherese people. Still, there's a certain amount of distrust between the races. The phaerimm have heard a rumor that illithids are merely mutated humans who've undergone severe physical changes because of their diet. Apparently, early humans thrown into the Underdark were forced to feed upon whatever they found, and one such food creature was the intellect devourer. If this is true, a human can become an illithid simply by consuming an intellect devourer; is it possible to reverse this change?

Rumors After the Fall

Characters who seek to continue adventuring in the remnants of Netheril can continue exploring the fragments of that society. Many of the rumors and fears of the survivors are unfounded, the product of nightmares brought on by long days and nights of worrying for one's own survival as the survivors of the Fall set up new kingdoms.

☞ An arcanist from one of the old enclaves was working on a completely new style of magic before the Fall and is in the process of setting up a brand new enclave with it. The source of the magical power will be even more potent than a *mythallar*, allowing quasimagical items to function at ten times the distances of before. This arcanist is planning to create the most massive enclave Netheril has ever seen and rule the entire nation from it.

The DM can use this hook in one of several ways. The information could actually be true, and the arcanist might hire groups of adventures to spread the word and encourage the people of Netheril to flock to him and return to the life they knew and loved. The arcanist might also need protection from rival arcanists who want the secrets of this new form of magic, or from the phaerimm, who obviously do not want to see the arcanists get back into power.

Alternatively, the arcanist might be particularly unpleasant and has hired thugs to act as press gangs and force citizens to join this new enclave. The heroes then might be urged to protect the common folk from these thugs. Other arcanists might hire the PCs to help them steal the new magic or to destroy it.

If the information is only a rumor, there is still quite a bit of chaos that will certainly ensue, and the characters might get caught up in something of a "range war" between former arcanists who each think their rivals have this new magic. The phaerimm might show up *en mass* and begin seeking out this new form of magic by whatever means they deem necessary. In fact, one of the rumors might be that this new type of magic is so radically different that it is undetectable by the phaerimm. This would certainly cause that race to take drastic action.

☞ The second set of the *nether scrolls* are being brought back to the ruins of Karsus's enclave in order to revive magic. Again, the competition amongst the arcanists would be fierce, and the phaerimm would get in on the act, too.

☞ Karsus is alive and well and is traveling incognito to other parts of the world. The Fall was actually masterminded by him as a means of escaping his duties as head of the enclave—he was sick and tired of the day-to-day issues that constantly interrupted his work. Karsus is truly dead, but this new impostor shares many of Karsus's attributes, including an uncanny knack at spellcasting. A former student of Karsus, the young man was somehow altered by the magical forces of the Karsus Enclave at the time of the Fall—and he truly believes that he is Karsus (and so does everyone else who meets him).

"Karsus" might ask the heroes to join him as he travels far away, fearing that if others notice who he is, they would wish to exact revenge upon him. Conversely, they might interact with him without ever realizing who they speak with, and only later learn the truth. The PCs might be asked to track the Archwizard down and bring him back to Netheril to face public wrath.

☞ The Lichlord survived the Fall and is hot to exact his revenge on anyone and everyone who was responsible for it. This could certainly include the characters, whether they aided Karsus in acquiring his spell components or not (and whether or not they defeated the Lichlord at the end of the adventure). Regardless of the conclusions the Lichlord drew before the Fall, he may have rethought them now that this disaster has struck. Thus, he will make the characters' lives a living nightmare as he begins sending minions of all numbers and abilities to capture them and bring them before him, where he will personally mete out his retribution.

Even if characters were sure that they defeated the Lichlord, they could still be faced with his wrath. Perhaps his defeat merely catapulted his essence into the Negative Material Plane. He's made his way back to Netheril now to exact his revenge upon the heroes.

☞ The surviving arcanists are hearing rumors that the phaerimm are massing to the north, planning to complete the final step of their plan to annihilate the Netherese. Arcanists—even those highly protected by magical means and bodyguards—are disappearing at an alarming rate, the victims of the phaerimm's ruthless master plan.

In truth, the arcanists are being systematically killed off by the growing power of the thieves' guild. As player-characters investigate the disappearances, they discover an ever-growing influence of thieves and assassins. Soon, the PCs become embroiled in a power struggle within the survivor states.

If the heroes investigate north, they find themselves stuck in the middle of a battle between the sharn and the phaerimm. Both sides are unleashing the full force of their magic in an attempt to annihilate the other, and the geology of the land is mutating under the magical forces. The characters must discover a way to put an end to the war and get out alive.

Netherese Zombie

CLIMATE/TERRAIN:	Any
FREQUENCY:	Rare
ORGANIZATION:	Nil
ACTIVITY CYCLE:	Any
DIET:	Nil
INTELLIGENCE:	Avg (8-10)
TREASURE:	Nil
ALIGNMENT:	Neutral evil
NO. APPEARING:	2d8
ARMOR CLASS:	6
MOVEMENT:	9
HIT DICE:	6
THAC0:	15
NO. OF ATTACKS:	2
DAMAGE/ATTACK:	2d4/2d4
SPECIAL ATTACKS:	*Raise dead*, control undead
SPECIAL DEFENSES:	Spell immunities
MAGIC RESISTANCE:	Nil
SIZE:	M (6' tall)
MORALE:	Special
XP VALUE:	650

Netherese zombies are undead creatures resembling normal zombies that move about the surface of Netheril on various errands for their master, the Lichlord. While a few of these creatures are independent of their creator, most are known to serve the Lichlord in one manner or another.

These undead are frequently encountered wearing the same clothing as they did in life. It's not uncommon for Neth zombies to be wearing fine robes and jewelry, death shrouds, or other clothing that they happened to be wearing before they were converted into undeath.

There's a sparkling of intelligence in a Netherese zombie—the last vestige of humanity left in its body. Each zombie speaks whatever languages it knew in life (typically common) and also communicates telepathically with the Lichlord.

Combat: Neth zombies typically attack in force, seeking to overwhelm any opposition quickly. While a few servants of the Lichlord have been known to hurl daggers or flaming oil, most Neth zombies prefer the direct approach. Once a direct attack fails, however, the Lichlord is quick to inform other bands of his zombies to attack with ranged weapons, wait until night to attack, or simply ambush opponents. Netherese zombies are turned as spectres and attack during their normal Initiative (they don't always attack last in a round).

While engaged in melee, these zombies seek to pummel or claw their opponents to the ground. The Neth zombie that defeats an opponent can then choose to *raise dead* on that creature, transforming him into a Netherese zombie in 1d4 turns. As the transformation comes to fruition, the skin slowly turns a pale white, fingernails become sharp, and the eyes sink in a bit.

A successfully cast *remove curse* versus 12th-level magic stops the transformation, returning the victim to the ranks of the dead. From there, a normal *raise dead* or *resurrection* spell can be used to bring the creature back to life as described above after being defeated in combat. Zombies of Netherese variety can also control nonthinking undead (skeletons, normal zombies, and others) within 30 feet. Such control is equivalent to that of an evil priest who successfully controls undead. Neth zombies are immune to *sleep*, *charm*, *hold*, *death magic*, *poison*, and *cold-based* attacks. A vial of holy water inflicts 2d4 points of damage.

Habitat/Society: Most Netherese zombies are loyal servants to the Lichlord. These creatures roam the lands of Netheril searching for new recruits to add to the Lichlord's army of undead. Each zombie possesses a burning desire to kill any human it encounters.

Neth zombie retain most of their Intelligence (10 maximum) and the ability to speak. They also keep the personality and memories that they had in life, typically using these to their advantage in service to the Lichlord. Overall, creatures retain two-thirds of the abilities they had in life (so a fighter with 18 Strength would be reduced to a Strength of 12).

All of these undead answer only to the telepathic will of the Lichlord, though he may from time to time appoint a wraith or spectre to command in his stead.

Ecology: As zombies swell their ranks with those they defeat, it becomes increasingly difficult to oppose this wave of undead as it ravages the countryside. In short order, entire villages are absorbed into a growing mass of destruction that sweeps up anything it encounters. Fertile fields are trampled flat by their passing, and animals flee as they approach.

The FORGOTTEN REALMS® Campaign:
Adventure Awaits!

Deep dungeons beg exploration.
Vicious dragons dare adventurers to enter their lairs.
Lost treasures wait to be claimed.
And everywhere the forces of chaos and evil are spreading their influence.

This is the FORGOTTEN REALMS Campaign World:
a place of classic medieval adventure and legendary mystery—
and TSR's most popular world for the ADVANCED DUNGEONS & DRAGONS® Game.
Here a hero can wander for years and still not see everything.
It all starts with these products!

The basic materials required for game play in the Realms! The box includes four maps and three books with details on the land, peoples, and potential adventures.
FORGOTTEN REALMS Campaign Setting
TSR #1085
Sug. Retail $30.00
ISBN 1-56076-617-4

Everything you need to know about Waterdeep, the most splendid city in the Realms. Great adventures start with the details included in four books and six maps!
City of Splendors
Campaign Expansion
TSR #1109
Sug. Retail $25.00
ISBN 1-56076-868-1

The City of Splendors as seen through Volo's eyes! The lovable renegade's guidebook to Waterdeep offers a view to the seamier side of things.
Volo's Guide to Waterdeep
Accessory
TSR #9379
Sug. Retail $9.95
ISBN 1-56076-335-3

Delve deep below Waterdeep itself in the sequel to the classic Ruins of Undermountain adventure. Who knows what lurks far below the city?
Ruins of Undermountain II: The Deep Levels
Adventure
TSR #1104
Sug. Retail $25.00
ISBN 1-56076-821-5

Look for TSR games and books at your favorite store, or to find the location nearest you call toll-free 1-800-384-4TSR.
Questions? Call Rob Taylor at 414-248-2902.

® and ™ designate trademarks owned by TSR, Inc. ©1996 TSR, Inc. All rights reserved.